I0460391

VOLUME ONE

EVERNIGHT PUBLISHING ®

www.evernightpublishing.com

Copyright© 2025

ISBN: 978-0-3695-1287-1

Cover Artist: Jay Aheer

Editor: Lisa Petrocelli

ALL RIGHTS RESERVED

VOLUME ONE

Monsters of New York is a sizzling paranormal romance series where passion collides with danger in the heart of the city that never sleeps. Each book introduces a new, irresistible shifter—each with its own dark secrets and primal desires. From wolves and bears to elusive creatures lurking in the shadows, these powerful beings navigate love, loyalty, and mystery in a world filled with human and supernatural monsters.

Set against the backdrop of New York's vibrant streets and hidden corners, every romance is an unforgettable journey where forbidden love and heated encounters could be the death of them—or the one thing that saves them. With danger always just around the corner, the shifters must face not only the threats of their own kind but the intense pull of a love that could change everything.

Uncover the secrets, feel the heat, and discover if love can tame the wildest beasts in Monsters of New York.

VOLUME ONE

RUNNING WITH DIREWOLVES

Monsters of New York

Lily Harlem

Copyright © 2025

Chapter One

Sienna peered through the bars of the dark cage. The latest arrival into her care was a direwolf, and she could hardly believe she was looking at it in the flesh. The huge canine had been considered extinct since the Ice Age. She'd learned that at college when studying zoology, yet now here was one right before her. Its glacial blue eyes were piercing and its shoulders were over a meter from the ground. Never had she seen such a big wolf, or one that exuded such strength.

"Where have you been hiding?" she murmured as the creature continued to stare at her. "How did you evade humans for millennia?"

The wolf blinked, stood, and turned away, showing her its long dark back and thick tail.

It had been picked up in Montana by a ranger

checking on his cattle. How he'd done it without getting mauled was baffling, but she was grateful because now the beautiful, mysterious creature was here, in her zoo, in her canine compound.

The other wolves—the regular gray wolves—were howling from their enclosure next door. They had been since the direwolf had arrived. Clearly, they could sense it, smell it, and they were on edge. With a bit of luck, they'd get used to it after a few days and quiet down. Because the direwolf was staying. This was his new home and his new life. He would be their star attraction with visitors from all over the world and from every scientific discipline.

"Try and get some sleep," she said to the animal. "And I'll see you in the morning ready for your big reveal."

A huge press conference had been organized before the first visitors to Central Park Zoo were invited to see the famous new arrival. Sienna hoped the crowd wouldn't upset the precious direwolf further. He hadn't eaten since his capture three days ago and that worried her.

She once again checked the lock on the gate, secured the keys in her locker, then turned. A sense of remorse nipped at her. The majestic creature had been roaming free in the Rocky Mountains, minding its own business, and now it was locked up, and would be for the rest of its days. A team of zoologists were out in the mountains searching for more direwolves. There must be more, they said, a species had to breed. They'd also be locked up when captured. Perhaps her direwolf would be happier when he had company.

"Good night, Ted." Sienna waved at the night guard who was sitting in his office by the staff entrance. The glow of screens lit his face. "Have a good one."

"I will if your wolves pipe down." He poked his finger in his ear.

"They will, hopefully." She chuckled and slipped her purse strap over her head.

She took a well-lit path toward the main road and decided a drink would settle the uneasy feeling about the direwolf's capture.

The Gin Room was her usual haunt after a long day. She slipped through the door illuminated by the neon pink sign above it, and made her way to the bar. "Bombay with elderflower tonic," she said with a smile to the barman.

"Coming right up, Sienna." He reached for a glass. "Good day?"

"Not bad, you?"

"New kid dropped a crate of glasses but other than that..." He tutted as he poured. "You got that direwolf at your place?"

"Yes."

"Thought you would have, you work in the wolf bit, right?"

"Yes, I'm head keeper of the canines."

"What's it like? The dire?"

"Big. Bright blue eyes."

"I can't wait to see it."

"You will soon." She took her drink and set down a few bills. "Thanks for this, I need it."

"No worries." He smiled and moved on to another customer.

Sienna glanced around. The bar was half full. A mixture of couples and groups of friends. She found a seat in a booth and was glad to get the weight off her feet. It had been a long day.

Pulling out her phone, she checked her emails. Several journalists had reached out directly about the direwolf as well as a TV news channel. She ignored them, the zoo's marketing department handled that stuff. Her priority was the welfare of her animals.

She sipped her drink and thought of the direwolf. His eyes brimmed with intelligence, as though he knew something she didn't, as though he understood things she never could. His lack of appetite concerned her. Was it because he was scared? Maybe it was a protest hunger strike. How could she tempt him to eat? Had they presumed his natural diet was the same as other wolves, or did he have a different set of nutritional requirements?

"Can I sit here?"

Sienna looked up at the sound of a deep voice. A tall guy, early twenties, dressed all in black, nodded at the opposite side of her booth.

"Oh … I…" She looked around.

"There's nowhere else," he said and took a slug from a bottle of beer.

It was true. The Gin Room had suddenly gotten busy. "Sure, go ahead." She smiled and went back to her phone, bringing up a research paper on wolf nutrition in the hope of solving her problem.

The man sat, he was quiet as he poked at the label on his beer, perhaps listening to the jazz playing from speakers. After about twenty minutes he spoke, "Want another?" He nodded at her empty glass.

"I…" She studied him. He was young and handsome, there was no denying that. He had a long straight nose and a dimple in the center of his chin. His jawline held a shadow of stubble and his eyes were piercing blue, just like the direwolf's.

"No strings." He shrugged. "I'm just going to the bar and it's busy up there now."

"Okay, thanks, I'll give you some money." She didn't want to be indebted.

"My treat." He stood and walked away.

For a moment her attention lingered on his jean-clad ass. It was damn cute and a perfect handful.

It had been a long time since she'd had any bedroom action. Since splitting with Graham, she'd thrown herself into work. Her friend Mae kept telling her to get back in the saddle, even if it was just a one-night stand. Maybe she should. Maybe Beer Guy could come in useful. Scratch the itch. No … he was too young. She had to be fifteen years his senior.

She squirmed on her seat as she watched him at the bar. His shoulders were wide and his light brown hair licked the base of his neck. Beneath those clothes was a damn fine body—she'd bet good money on that.

A couple of girls to his right were checking him out, nudging each other. He turned, drinks in hand, and wandered back, appearing not to notice his admirers.

Quickly she studied her phone again.

"Here." He slid a gin and tonic her way. "I asked the barman what you drank."

"Ah, thanks. Yes, he knows. I pop in often enough."

"Nice to have a regular place."

"I guess." She paused as he sat. "You from the city?"

"No, just visiting."

"Work?"

"Something like that."

"Man of mystery, eh?"

He kind of smiled and took a drink of his beer.

Sienna set down her phone. "So, if you're visiting, have you done the tourist sights?"

"You mean the Empire State?"

"Yes, that, and Statue of Liberty, Central Park…"

"I've been in the park all day."

"And did you enjoy it?"

"Busy, I'm not used to so many people."

"That's the Big Apple for you." She glanced at the two girls who'd been regarding her drink companion. They were wandering off. "What's your name?"

"Tarl. You?"

"Sienna." Tarl, that was an unusual name. It suited him, though. There was something curious about him but she couldn't put her finger on what.

"You live here, Sienna?"

"Yes, just around the corner." She glanced at his ring finger. It was empty. Of course it was, at his age he hadn't had time to find the love of his life.

"Not sure if I could do the city full time." He scooted along a bit so he was directly opposite her. "I like open space."

"Room to roam, right?"

He chuckled. "Yeah, exactly that."

"So how long are you staying?"

"I'll be out of here soon … I hope."

Ah, so if she wanted some fun there was no time to waste. She sipped her drink and studied his face. Did an age gap really matter if it was just a one-night stand?

He was looking at her with equal interest. There was sparkle in the depths of his eyes and his lips were damp where he'd just licked them.

Was he thinking the same as her? Was he thinking about sex and wondering just how good they'd be together? If so, there was only one way to find out.

"Wanna get out of here?" she said, feeling both bold and nervous. He might cut her down, tell her she was too old. Reject her the way Graham had. But life was too short not to take a chance.

He raised his right eyebrow. "What you got in mind?"

"I've had a long day, my brain is frazzled. I could really do with some fun."

"Fun?" He leaned forward, elbows on the table. "Fun of the bedroom variety?"

"It would be more comfortable than the back-alley variety."

He smiled. "To tell you the truth, I've been damn stressed too, some fun sounds like a good antidote."

Her heart rate picked up. She hadn't read the signals wrong, thank goodness. She took a few big gulps of her drink and slipped her phone into her purse. "Can you promise me you're not a serial killer or a terrorist?"

"I'm many things, Sienna, but neither of those." He finished his beer and banged it on the table. "I'm also quite capable of taking you back to my hotel room if you don't want me to invade your space."

Having Tarl invade her space was all she could really think about. It was what she wanted suddenly. "I live a few doors from here. Add not being a thief to that list and you are cordially invited."

"I'm no thief."

"Good."

He stood and held out his hand. He really was very tall, his limbs long, and his pants sat low on his hips, his abdomen flat as a board. She took his hand, his flesh warm against hers, and stood.

The barman glanced their way and an expression of surprise crossed his face. He'd never seen Sienna leave with someone before and it clearly was notable. If Tarl turned out to be a freaking weirdo, at least there was a witness to who she'd left with.

Stepping outside, she shook that feeling. Tarl radiated a sense of calm confidence that was very attractive and reassuring and was unusual in such a young man.

It was raining lightly and a cab passed, its tires splashing in the puddles. Tarl switched sides with her, so if there was any stray water it would hit him and not her.

She glanced over the road at the park. She thought of the direwolf, and hoped he was at least trying to eat some of the meat she'd left out for him.

"This is me," she said after just a minute.

"You weren't lying, you really do live close to The Gin Room."

She smiled, took out her key, and opened the door.

They paused in the tiny hallway that led to her small living space with a sofa, a bed behind a curtain, and a small functional kitchen. It was warm and smelled of the jasmine reed stick she'd set on a shelf. When she shut the front door, silence wrapped around them.

She swallowed and looked up at Tarl. Shadows enveloped his face as he leaned down and cupped her cheeks.

"How'd you wanna do this?" he murmured.

"Do what?"

"Do you want me to seduce you?" he asked. "Or just get to the business of fucking?"

"Can I get both?"

He grinned. "Sure thing." His mouth brushed over hers, a gentle kiss that tasted of beer.

She gripped the material of his slightly coarse sweater and pressed in close. He was warm and smelled of the outdoors. He moaned slightly and pulled her closer, his embrace firm and full of desire.

Sienna closed her eyes and gave herself up to him. It had been so long since she'd enjoyed any kind of passion and now her body craved joining with another.

He pulled back and knotted his fingers with hers. "This way, right?"

"Yes."

He tugged her forward a few steps and flicked on the overhead light. Sienna blinked in the harshness and quickly drew the curtains and turned on a table lamp with a red shade that gave a softer glow.

Tarl turned off the overhead light and sat. He bent and began to undo the laces on his thick black boots that looked more suitable for a mountain hike than the city.

His sweater stretched over his shoulders, his hair hung forward, and his long elegant fingers worked efficiently.

Damn, she'd gotten lucky. Her day had really taken a turn for the better.

VOLUME ONE

Chapter Two

"Seduction means me undressing you, right?" Tarl said, peeling off his sweater and throwing it to one side.

Sienna blew out the match she was holding, she'd just lit a rose candle. "I … I'm gonna take a shower. I've been at work all day." Fuck, without his clothes the guy was even better than she'd imagined. He had the perfect amount of dark body hair over smooth golden skin and a true six-pack. He was muscle-bound, but not gym muscle, it was from physical work. He was a man who used his body the way evolution had intended.

"Want company?" he asked, glancing at the bathroom. The door was open.

"That would make a nice change." She kicked off her sneakers, went into the bathroom, and flicked on the water.

"So, when was the last time you shared a shower?" he asked following her.

"Personal question." She peered in the mirror to remove her earrings.

"We're about to get real personal so what does that matter?"

She smiled at his reflection. "True."

He came up behind her, wrapped his hands around her waist, and nuzzled into the curve of her neck. "You sure about this?"

"Yes."

"'Cause if you're having second—"

"I'm not." She paused and ran her hand over his hair-coated forearm. "And it's been over a year. Bad breakup and all that, he was a cheat, I threw myself into work."

"I'm sorry." He frowned and his mouth flattened. "Really, that's tough."

"Don't be sorry. He wasn't the one for me."

"Can I be? Tonight at least?" He pulled a lock of hair over her shoulder. His touch was delicate and gentle.

For a moment she wondered about pointing out their age difference but held it in. There was no point spoiling the mood. "I'd like that, Tarl. Tonight at least."

He kissed the shell of her ear and set about opening the buttons on her shirt. When they were undone, he slipped the material from her shoulders and undid her bra. The cups loosened and still looking in the mirror she watched as her breasts were exposed.

Tarl was watching too, and when the bra had been dropped to the floor, forgotten, he cupped her breasts in his big hands. She moaned and let her head fall back onto him. It was so good to be touched.

"You're beautiful," he whispered, his breath warm on her cheek. "So beautiful."

She appreciated his words. He was a guy who could have any woman, likely both pretty girls at the bar at the same time, yet he'd come home with her. Destiny or fate, or the alignment of stars, had worked in her favor for once.

"I want to worship your body," he said. "Slowly, starting here and working my way down."

The mirror was steaming up and she spun in his arms. "That sounds like a plan I could get onboard with."

He grinned, a seriously sexy, almost feral grin, and shoved at his pants.

Sienna pushed at her cargo trousers and stepped from them and her panties.

"To tell the truth," he said, his cock springing free from his boxers. "Been a while since I was with a woman too."

She tipped her head. "Does that mean you've been with a man?"

He laughed. "Would that bother you?"

"No." She took his hand and stepped into the running water. "Not in the least. Two guys together are hot."

"*You're* hot." He circled his arm around her waist and pulled her in for another kiss.

This one was more urgent, and his erection was trapped between their bodies. She roamed her hands over his flesh, learning his shape, the expanse of his shoulders, and the dips and rises of his biceps.

"Need soaping up?" he asked onto her lips.

"Sure." She reached for the shower gel.

He filled his palms with fragrant white suds and began to smooth them over her body, paying particular attention to her breasts, her ass, and the tops of her thighs. When his fingers slipped between her legs she gripped his shoulders. "Oh … yes…"

"You're perfection," he said. "Exquisite."

"No, I'm not … but you are." His wet body shone and small drips sat on his long eyelashes.

"Huh, I'm just a hairy guy."

"A fit, hairy guy." She stroked down his abdomen and took hold of his cock.

He gritted his teeth and his shaft jerked in her hand. "Careful with that, it's ready to go."

"So shall we take our fun to bed?"

"No." His eyes flashed. "This will do."

Suddenly she was in the air, her back against the cool shower wall, and her legs wrapped around his waist. "Tarl!"

"We've got all night, haven't we?"

"Yes." She nodded and was aware of his cock

probing her entrance. "We have."

"Good." His body was tense, desire fizzing from him. "'Cause this will just be orgasm number one."

Oh, she liked the sound of that. "Yes, fuck me, now … here…"

He pushed in, staring into her eyes as his cock stretched her pussy. It was a slow wet ride and she savored every inch of him. When he reached full depth, a long low groan rumbled from his chest and his balls pressed up against her.

"Fuck, yes," she said, dragging her hands through his wet hair. "That feels good."

His mouth hit down and he ground his body up against hers.

Her toes curled and her pussy clenched as the pressure increased on her clit. He was getting the angle just right each time he thrust his hips.

"Oh … more," she gasped against his lips. "Give me more."

It was as though she'd shown a red rag to a bull. He let out an animalistic growl and withdrew, only to blast back in with an upward lunge.

She cried out, the sensation exquisite, and locked her arms around his neck. This was going to be one hell of a ride.

"You okay?" he asked gruffly.

"Yes. Yes. Don't stop."

She felt wild and wanton. When had she ever been so crazed with lust? Invited a handsome young stranger back and got naked in minutes? Never. But it felt so good. She was high. High on sex and the need to climax.

Their wet bodies slid together as he pounded into her over and over. The orgasm was racing toward her, it was going to be hard and fast and breath-stealing. It was like an explosion just waiting to happen.

"Oh, yes…" She wailed, the sound echoing around the small bathroom. "That's it, just there … don't … I need…"

He knew just what she needed and he upped the pace, increased the pressure on her clit. She came, a near violent burst of sensation that blasted through her body. The pleasure gushed from her, a hot outburst of release.

"Fuck. Yes." He came with her, pushing the air from her lungs as he drove into her as though he couldn't get deep enough.

Her wet body shook as she spasmed around his cock. Her skin tingled and her pulse roared in her ears.

His release extended and his chest pressed against hers as his fingers curled into her ass, holding her just where he wanted her. There'd be bruises tomorrow but she didn't care. This was just what she'd needed, tonight of all nights.

"In the name of…" he gasped against her temple and stilled. "That was incredible."

"I know." She closed her eyes, her breaths still hard to catch. "And just the first … right?"

"Yeah." He released her right buttock and stroked her sopping hair. "Just the first." He grinned. "You reckon you can stay up all night doing that?"

"The question is…" She laughed. "Can you?"

"Hell, yeah." He pulled out and set her feet on the shower tray. "I've got no problems with stamina."

Damn, she really should have considered dating a younger guy years ago. His cock was still hard and fully erect. It was going to be a great night.

She stepped under the water and held her face up to the flow. Warmth slipped down her inner thigh. She was glad she'd continued to take the pill. It meant she had no worries about pregnancy if an exciting night like this one happened to come along.

He grabbed a blob of shampoo, scrubbed it over his hair, and then stepped under the water. "All of your stuff smells of flowers."

"I guess so." She stepped out and reached for a fluffy white towel.

"I like it." He rinsed his hair then flicked off the water.

"Here." She handed him a towel and then wandered from the bathroom.

"So, where's the bed?" he asked, following her.

"Hidden, behind here." She pulled back a heavy red curtain. "Makes it cozy."

"Sure does." He nodded.

"Want a drink?"

"Just water, please."

She filled two glasses.

He took several gulps then a photograph she'd taken of the pack of gray wolves in her care caught his attention. "That's good."

"Thanks."

"You take it?"

"Yes. They're beautiful, don't you think?"

"No, snappy, bad tempered, not the brightest of sparks."

"What?" She gave a shocked laugh. Everyone loved wolves, well, everyone she knew anyway. "Why would you say that?"

He shrugged. "I try and avoid them."

"And do you have to avoid them often?"

"When I'm home, yeah."

"And home is? You didn't say."

"No, I didn't." His attention moved to a picture of Samba, the poodle she'd owned growing up. "I've been in Montana lately."

"Nice. Wild."

"Yep, and big. Suits us … usually."

"Us?"

"Yeah, my family, you know."

She frowned at him. "What do you mean, usually?"

He used the towel to scrub his hair then tossed it onto the back of a chair. "Usually, we are left alone. But lately … let's just say we've had some unwanted visitors."

"And that's why you've come to New York? Because of the visitors?"

He walked up to her, utterly naked and still deliciously aroused. "I don't want to talk about them. I want to continue exploring your sexy little body."

"You do?" She licked her lips and stared into his blue eyes. "Right now?"

"Yeah, right now." He gathered her close, the towel fell away, and he kissed her.

As his tongue stroked hers, he moved her to the bed and flicked back the curtain. The next thing Sienna knew she was flat on her back with a big, hot guy kissing her, and his cock nudging up against her.

She'd just had one orgasm but her greedy body craved more and she arched her back offering herself up to him. Thoughts of Montana and unwanted visitors fled her mind. All she could think of was Tarl and how his body felt over hers.

"So sweet," he murmured, kissing down her neck then taking her right nipple into his mouth.

"Oh, yes…" She stroked his hair as her nipple tightened and her breast ached with longing.

He cupped her left breast, tweaking that nipple as he worked the other. The heat coming off him was intense, and his desire was palpable.

His kisses spread lower, traveling over her abdomen and dipping into her navel. His hands were everywhere, stroking her hips, her waist, her inner thighs, and when he dipped his head to her pussy, she spread her legs, hoping he was going to give her oral.

"This one is going to take a while," he said, looking up at her with hooded eyes. "No rush, enjoy the journey."

Her pussy quivered with anticipation.

"I know I'm going to enjoy it," he said huskily, "every fucking second."

He stroked his tongue through the soft damp folds of her pussy. She moaned and closed her eyes, fisted the duvet cover. It had been so long she couldn't even remember when she'd last been adored like this.

Tarl got to work, steady strokes of his tongue over her clit while gently probing her entrance with his fingers. Not enough to tip her over the edge but enough to have her writhing for more.

"Oh … please…" she moaned after ten minutes. "I want to…"

"I'll decide that." He grinned up at her. "But it won't be long now, I can taste your desperation."

"Please … I…" Her thighs were trembling with longing and her belly tight with need.

He closed his eyes and worked her clit again applying a little more pressure but still not enough. He began to finger-fuck her deeper, stroking over her G-spot each time he rode in.

"Oh God." She arched her back and bunched her fingers in his hair. "That's it … please … just…"

He kept her balanced there. Maddeningly close to release but unable to tip over the edge. She squirmed and bucked and tugged at her nipples. "Tarl! Oh, you're driving me insane."

Suddenly he gripped her ass cheek with his free hand and sucked her clit as he flicked it with his tongue, a fast urgent rhythm that took her straight to the precipice of orgasm. She cried out, pulled her knees up to hug his shoulders, and ground against his face.

His fingers mimicked a thick cock fucking her and she let the dense sensation flood her pussy and came hard and long. He stayed with her, his mouth on her clit and his nose buried in her pubic hair.

On and on the spasms wrecked her, shaking her body and stealing her breath. His fingers moved through her wetness. She was so wet, much more than usual. "Oh God..." she moaned, the density of the pleasure was insane.

"Fuck," he said, looking up at her, his mouth and chin shiny. "You really are a squirter."

"What!" She pushed to her elbows, her breasts hitching up and down with her rapid breaths. Her pussy was still convulsing around his fingers.

"You're a squirter," he said again. "And it's fucking hot."

"I ... I am not."

"Oh, you are." He withdrew from her pussy and swiped the palm of his hand over her soft folds. "You're soaking and it came out in a gush as you orgasmed."

"Oh my God," she moaned, her cheeks reddening. "I'm sorry. I-I don't know why ... or what?"

"Hey." He came up over her and set his lips on hers. "I'm not complaining, hell, I love it. Proves I hit the spot."

"But I've never ... before." She stared into his eyes, trying to see if he was telling the truth about her copious wetness turning him on.

He gave a truly self-satisfied grin. "That's 'cause you've never had me lick your pussy, babe. That's why you've never squirted before."

"You are good with your tongue."

"I know." He sat back, straddling her, and took hold of his cock. "Now it's my turn. Like this." With his free hand he pressed her right breast upward and inward.

She knew what he wanted, he wanted her to hold herself so he could come on her chest. A rush of excitement went through her at the thought of watching him masturbate right there before her eyes.

Chapter Three

Tarl was on a mission. Sienna could see that. He was working his cock with industrious movements, not speedy and not slow, clearly just the pace and tension he enjoyed the most.

His belly was taught and his breaths were coming fast and shallow. His eyes flashed as he stared at her breasts, practically unblinking as he watching her tweak her nipples and arch her back.

"It's all for you," she murmured, wondering if he was the sort who liked dirty words. "My tits are for you, come on them, I want to see you come, Tarl."

"Ah, fuck, yeah…" He sped up, sliding his thumb over his deep slit.

"Don't stop," she said, "come on me, spurt your cum on me. Fuck, yeah, come, Tarl."

He groaned and gritted his teeth and then he sped up, as though having decided not to hold off his orgasm anymore.

Her heart rate was tripping along, the shadows basting his body made him all the sexier, like some kind of Roman God—a statue of Romulus she'd seen once.

"Ah, fuck, yeah, yeah." He closed his eyes, tipped his head back, the tendons on his neck straining, and came.

Pearly cum spilled from his cock, landing on her breasts and coating her right hand.

"That's it," she murmured, rubbing the warm fluid over her right nipple. "Come like that, more."

He did, another slap of cum accompanied by his deep primitive groan of satisfaction.

"Mm, fuck, that's hot." He opened his eyes and

looked down at her. "You look amazing like that … covered in my spunk."

"You're a tits man, huh?" She grinned up at him.

"When it's your tits, yeah, seems that way." He flopped down next to her. "You have a great body, Sienna. The fucking best."

A flush of pleasure went through her. Tarl didn't seem to notice their age difference. Her breasts weren't quite as perky as they had been and her hips a little wider than when she'd been in her early twenties, but what the hell. He clearly liked what he saw.

"But I'm not done with you," he said breathlessly. "I'll have you orgasming again before morning."

"I'll hold you to that." She reached for a Kleenex and wiped her chest. Then she pulled the duvet up over them. "But I need a few minutes to recover first."

"Me too." He chuckled and hugged her close. "But come here and let me hold you, you're warm and soft and smell so damn nice."

She allowed herself to be scooped into his strong warm embrace and breathed in the hot scent of his skin. She sighed, enjoying their connection, flesh on flesh, the absolute maleness of him.

When she awoke it was to the sound of her alarm.

"What the fuck?" She sat and blinked. Had it all been a dream?

No, to her left was Tarl. He was flat on his back, mouth slightly parted and his hair messy over the white pillowcase.

He blinked open his eyes. "Damn, is it morning?"

"Yes." She switched off her alarm by banging the top of it.

"Fuck, we never got to go for another round of fun." He reached for her. "But no time like the present."

She giggled and pushed him away. "It would be

great, but I have to get to work."

"They can wait."

"No, I have animals relying on me. I can't be late. Never have been and never will be."

"Animals?"

Sienna wriggled from his eager arms and flicked back the curtain that screened the bed from her tiny living space. "I have to shower."

"Want company?"

"I'd love that … another time maybe."

"Spoilsport."

"You make coffee." Quickly she shut the bathroom door and flicked on the shower.

Within minutes she was clean and dry and pulling on her combats and a fresh black sweater with the Central Park Zoo logo on the front. She then dragged a red hoodie over her head and eased out the knots in her hair.

"Caffeine." Tarl handed her a mug as she reappeared.

"Perfect, thanks." She walked to the window.

He'd opened the curtains and came to stand at her side holding a steaming mug of coffee.

"You have a great view of the park."

"I know, it's one of the reasons I took the apartment. I gave up square footage to be able to see the zoo." She pointed to the few dark structures poking above the tree line.

"The zoo?"

"Yes."

"You like the zoo? You know the zoo?" He turned to her with a frown.

She laughed. "Sure, I work there."

His mouth hung open a little. "Fuck."

"Why fuck?"

He shoved his hand through his hair causing it to

stick up. "I knew I was drawn to you … wasn't sure if … but you work there? At the zoo?"

She tipped her head and studied him. "Yes, why?" This was a most unusual reaction.

"Have you seen the direwolf?"

"You heard about that?"

"Hell, yes." He set down his coffee and took her hand. His eyes flashed with urgency. "Have you seen him?"

"Yes. He's in my care."

Tarl swallowed, his Adam's apple dipping low on his stubbled neck. "In your care." He paused. "He hasn't eaten, has he?"

"How do you know that?"

"I just do." He glanced at the door. "Are you going to work now?"

She took another sip of coffee. "Yes, if I want to be on time."

"Can I come with you?"

"What? To my work?"

"To the zoo, to see the direwolf." He squeezed her hand tighter and stepped close. "Please, Sienna. Please."

"But why?"

"Doesn't everyone want to see the creature that was considered extinct?"

"Yes, they do. And I have a press conference to prepare for, and more importantly, ensure the direwolf isn't stressed any more than he is. Everyone around the world wants to see him, everyone wants a piece of him, literally."

"A piece of him?"

"A strand of hair, a few cheek cells. His DNA is highly prized."

Tarl crumpled up his face as though in pain. "That's disgusting."

"That's what happens with a find of this magnitude."

"But the poor creature…"

She sighed and cupped his cheek. "I agree, and it's why I'm glad he's in my care. I have the power to protect him, to be his advocate, make sure he isn't treated like some test tube laboratory experiment."

"I'm so glad it's you." He set his warm hand over hers. "Please, let me come with you, to see him, just for a moment."

"It's important to you?" She could see it was, hear it was.

"More than you can ever imagine."

"Then get dressed, I'm leaving now." She finished her coffee and set the mug in the sink.

As she put on her boots, Tarl dragged on his sweater and stamped into his boots.

Soon they were crossing the street and heading down the alley that led under two park tunnels and toward the zoo. Autumn was encroaching and the first of the leaves had fallen and collected in small piles along the way.

"You have gray wolves at the zoo, right?" Tarl asked as it came into view.

"Yes. You saw the photo. You don't like them, do you?"

"No, and neither will the direwolf."

"How do you know that?"

"I have an interest in wolves and I know that different species of wolves, foxes, coyotes, avoid each other. They find their scents and their howls repugnant."

"Really? I didn't know that."

"It's a fact."

"Gosh, I learn something every day." She used her pass to swipe into the staff entrance. "Hi, Ted, hope you had a good night."

"Huh." He stood. "I'll be glad to get home for some peace. Your wolves have been at it all night. Kept half the city awake I should think." He looked at Tarl. "Who is this?"

"A friend, and a visitor. I'll sign him in." She reached for the logbook and a pen. "He's not staying long."

Ted shrugged.

Tarl, without a word, wrote his name in the book, his first name only, and no contact number. She frowned at him.

"I don't have a phone," he said, "never had the need."

She paused. "Really?"

"Yeah." He shrugged.

"Fair enough." But it was odd. How would she contact him if she wanted another round of fun? "This way."

She led him into another room where they stepped through a footbath to clean the base of their boots, and then she collected her keys from the locker.

Tarl was straining to look through a window. He was clearly very keen to see the direwolf.

The moment they stepped outside the howls of the gray wolves pierced the air with more gusto.

Tarl winced and downturned his mouth. "Bunch of whiners."

"It is a noise," she agreed. She opened a large metal gate that allowed her to access the backs of the enclosures. "No wonder Ted has had enough."

Tarl overtook her, walking fast, his paces purposeful and urgent. "He's this way." He hadn't said it as a question.

Soon they were at the direwolf's enclosure. Tarl

stepped straight up to the wire caging, hooked his fingers through it, and pressed his face to the metal.

"Hey, step back," Sienna said, scouring the shadows for the creature. "He's dangerous. He might lunge at you."

Suddenly she spotted two blue eyes, and then the direwolf emerged. He was as huge as ever, his every movement controlled and strong.

"There you are," Tarl said, his voice softening. "What the fuck happened back there, eh?"

The creature's attention was locked on Tarl. It kept walking toward him, his shoulder bones rolling with each step.

"Tarl," she said again. "Please, step back."

Once more he ignored her.

And then in a sudden movement, the direwolf bounded forward. It reached Tarl and stretched up against the cage so its head was higher than Tarl's.

Sienna gasped and rushed to him, tugged at his waist, trying to peel him away. But it was no good, he was too strong, too fixed into position.

"Tarl, he'll…"

"He won't hurt me," Tarl said, poking his fingers through to touch the direwolf's chin. "He just wants to get out of here. This isn't where he belongs."

Sienna froze and watched the interaction. The direwolf certainly seemed to have made an instant connection with Tarl. It couldn't stop staring at him, its intelligent eyes almost pleading for help.

Her belly tightened and once again she felt guilty that she held the keys to this creature's captivity. If only he hadn't been caught by that ranger and had continued to live in the wild. His discovery was great for science but it wasn't great for him.

"I know you're not eating," Tarl said. "But you

must, you'll need your strength."

The direwolf bared its teeth and growled.

"I promise, eat something."

The direwolf lunged backward and landed on all fours again.

"Please," Tarl said. "I absolutely promise, on my life."

"What do you promise?" Sienna asked, setting her hand on Tarl's shoulder. He seemed genuinely upset and anxious.

He shook his head, stepped back, and looked at her. "He shouldn't be in here. It's a crime, a terrible crime. He needs to roam free. You have to help him."

She frowned. In the past she'd come across zoo protestors, and most of the time she agreed with their arguments. But some animal captivity was to protect the species. The greatest good for the greatest number.

"I can't help him be free. He'll live out his days in captivity."

"No! That can't happen." Anger and frustration flashed in Tarl's eyes. "I beg you."

"It's not up to me, Tarl." She glanced behind herself, wondering if the new shift of security guards were about to do a round. "And he's been brought here for his own good."

"How is it for his own good? Last week he was wild and free, happy. And now he is depressed and starving and—"

"I'm sorry, Tarl, but you need to go now. I have things to do, plus the vet will be here soon to check him over before the press conference and…"

"Okay, okay." He scrubbed his hand over his stubbled cheek. "I get it. I get it." He turned back to the cage. "I'll figure something out. I will."

The direwolf sat and stared at him with his chin

tipped. Almost as if saying, "I'll be here waiting, go get on with it."

"I'm sorry, I can see you feel passionate about this and—"

"Sienna." Tarl's voice had quieted. "You have no idea how I feel about this."

And with that he strode away, back past the cages and to the gate. Then he was gone.

She looked at the direwolf. "You have quite the fan there, don't you?"

He tipped his head, his attention on her absolute.

"And get ready for a whole load more," she said. "The entire world wants to see you."

****

Sienna's day was a whirlwind of activity. There was the vet who was concerned about weight loss, then the press conference in which she'd been nominated as speaker, and a bunch of local dignitaries to meet, then the zoo's board members who were full of questions and a crowd of excited schoolchildren.

Although she'd been polite and engaging, her stress levels had gone up as the hours had gone by. The direwolf was very unhappy and not enjoying the people and the cameras. The howls of the gray wolves were a constant background noise and a few times she'd seen him hang his head as though utterly despairing of his situation.

When it came time for her to go home, Ted was back on duty.

"I am sorry about this noise," she said. "I gave them extra dinner to shut them up."

"Didn't work, did it?" He pulled out a couple of earplugs and dropped them on top of his book. "But I have come prepared." He sat at his screens. "So, all good."

"Very sensible." She touched his shoulder. "See you in the morning."

"You be careful out there, it's dark already now the clocks have changed."

"I haven't far to go."

Chapter Four

Sienna zipped her hoodie up to her chin and strode out into the darkness. Overhead the stars had dotted the sky and the honks of cabs sounded a long way off through the trees.

She made for her usual alleyway, frustrated when two of the lampposts weren't lit. Quickening her pace, she glanced around. It was a walk she'd done a hundred times and more, but still the park tunnels freaked her out a little when it was dark. She blamed some horror movie she'd watched years ago.

The scent of mulch hung in the damp air and something above her, a squirrel most likely, shook a branch. Bracing for the tunnel, she considered sprinting through it but resisted. It would be okay. It always had been before.

"Hey you. Stop!" a deep voice and a flash of silver.

Her heart stuttered and adrenaline shot into her system. "What the?" She gasped and clenched her fists.

"I've seen you on the TV today, you're rich, hand it over."

A tall man wearing a black hoodie pulled up tight so all she could really see was his nose and a dark moustache, emerged from the shadows.

"What? I'm not rich. I'm not on TV." She took a step backward.

He followed her. "Purse. Now."

"I don't have one!"

He spat and stepped closer with a long sharp knife waving in front of him. "Don't lie, all girls have a purse."

"I only have a phone." She reached into her

pocket.

"Give it." He went to snatch it from her.

But at that moment a rush of energy and movement came from behind her. It scooted around her shoulder and in a flash of fur and teeth pummeled into her attacker and knocked him to the floor. The knife skittered out of sight and his shrill scream filled the tunnel.

Sienna gasped and staggered backward until her shoulders hit the brick wall.

What the hell?

A wolf—a direwolf—was standing over the hooded man and snarling into his face, drool dripping from his menacing jaws.

"Argh! Get off me. Get off me!"

The creature lowered its head then snapped its teeth grazing the man's nose.

"Oh my God." Sienna pressed her hand to her mouth. How the hell had the direwolf escaped? But … was it even the same one? The tail on the one before her was much lighter, as were the ears. She could see that even through the darkness.

"Help! Help!"

Sienna had no intention of helping the man who had tried to mug her, perhaps even go on to stab her. With her body buzzing with fight-or-flight, she looked to her left. If only there was a cop around. This creature needed containing. It was wild and dangerous as was being proven right now and it could not be left to roam the streets of New York City.

There was a sudden scramble and the direwolf stepped back, seeming to allow the man to wriggle free. He took full advantage, jumped to his feet, and ran at full pelt into the darkness of the tunnel, his footsteps rapidly fading.

"Oh, fuck." Sienna gulped as the direwolf turned his attention to her. Had she evaded a mugging only to receive a mauling?

It came closer, slowly, its huge teeth on show and its hackles raised. It was staring straight at her with feral hunger in its blue eyes.

Now she knew it was a different direwolf. The markings were quite different and it was paler, white in places. But where the heck had it come from? And why here and now?

She splayed her hands on the damp bricks, she had no weapon and stood no chance of outrunning the creature. Her fate was sealed. She'd be forever known as the zookeeper mauled outside of the zoo.

Then something changed. For a moment she thought it was her vision going fuzzy, but then she realized it was the wolf's fur. It had turned hazy, fog-like. The animal lifted onto its back legs, human-style, and let out a long groan. Fur turned to skin. A wolf's snout became a man's nose and broad bare shoulders and lean hips became clear. The eyes stayed the same. And what was more, she recognized them. She recognized *him*.

"Tarl?" His name barely came out of her dry mouth. What had she just witnessed? Was this some elaborate joke? A hoax?

"Sienna." He stepped up to her. He wasn't wearing a scrap of clothing. "I'm sorry you went through that."

"Through what?" Her brain was having a hard time keeping up with events.

"That asshole," he said, jerking his head to the right. "With the knife."

"He's gone," she managed.

"And won't be back." He was so close now, and he pressed his hands to the wall either side of her head, hemming her in, looking down at her. "Because he knows I'll kill him."

"What … what was that? Who are you … and why … I don't understand?"

"No one would expect you to."

"Tarl, I…" Tentatively she pressed her hand to his warm chest. "Did you see the direwolf?"

He chuckled. "Babe, I *am* the direwolf."

She gulped. "Yes, I thought so."

"And I saved you from that thug."

"I know, thanks." His body heat was radiating onto her and his scent filled her lungs. "But you just changed from a direwolf to a human, that's impossible, I mean, I…"

"You graduated in zoology, yeah, you told me, but they don't know everything at these fancy colleges."

"One thing can't become another. It's a physical impossibility."

He raised one eyebrow, the way he had in the bar the night before. "Want me to do it again and show you just how possible it is?"

"Not right now." Her heart was pounding so hard she feared for its survival if she were subjected to much more. "But you did … you are…?"

"I'm a shifter, yes, a direwolf shifter, just the way Grady in there is." He nodded in the direction of the zoo. "Which is why we must get him out now."

"Oh my God." She cupped his face, feeling his very human bones beneath his flesh. "He's a … we have a man locked up? His name is Grady?"

"Yes, and he's a shifter, but he's also a man, all man in fact. Alpha male."

"I … I can't get my head around this."

"Then let me get dressed and we can figure it out."

"Figure it out?" Her brain was a mass of emotions and scientific questions.

"Yeah. Hang on." He disappeared for a second then returned with his battered rucksack.

As he dressed, she tried to catch her breath. The implications of what she knew were far-reaching, frightening, exciting, and gave her a huge ethical dilemma. She held the key that kept an innocent man locked up like an animal.

"Sienna." Tarl was dressed now and he took her hand. "You know we can't leave him in there. Caged."

"Why? I mean, why doesn't he just change into a human, if he can? Then anyone would release him, Ted on his rounds even."

"And let the world know shifters exist?" Tarl's eyes widened. "Are you crazy? Only a few people are privy to that information."

"And now I'm one of them."

"Yes." He steered her out of the tunnel, back in the direction of the zoo. "You're special, Sienna, I knew that the moment I saw you in The Gin Room. I didn't know how or why but I knew it."

"But Tarl, please, I'm figuring this out, please wait."

"We haven't time." He stopped and turned to her, placed his hands on her shoulders. "Grady is on a hunger strike. It's our final line of defense if caught by humans. We stop eating, die, and the secrets die with us." He paused and shook his head. "And as a direwolf he has an incredibly fast metabolic rate. A gray wolf could last three weeks without food, but Grady…" He paused and frowned. "Another day at the most."

"What?" Her heart squeezed. Die. No, they couldn't let him die.

"So come on," Tarl said, urging her to walk again.

"We don't have a moment to lose."

She kept up with him, her mind spinning. "Shifter? You're shifters? How many more of you are there?"

"All in good time." He looked left and right as they walked past the unlit lampposts. "I'll explain everything."

"I think I understand, it's how you've survived undetected for so long, right? You direwolves. You've been hiding in plain sight, walking amongst us."

He made a small huffing sound. "I knew you'd figure it out, and yes, we only shift, as a rule, when we're in the wilderness, no chance of discovery, except Grady and I were in Montana, hunting, and this ranger came out of nowhere. He darted Grady and hauled him onto his truck. I couldn't do a thing as a direwolf or as a man to help him." He shook his head. "I failed him."

"I'm sorry, I really am. But you're here now, so you haven't failed him at all." She steeled herself. There was only one thing she could do. Only one action that meant she'd be able to live with herself. She was an animal lover, a believer in freedom, every life mattered. "And you're about to free him, Tarl, with my help."

"Sienna." He stopped and cupped her cheeks. "Are you really going to help us?"

"What kind of human would I be if I didn't?"

"I don't know, but right now you are the most beautiful, bravest, kindest human I've ever met." He set his lips on hers. A lovely deep passionate kiss that brought back so many memories of the night before. "But you know this will be career suicide," he murmured. "I spotted the cameras in there earlier."

"And I'll be the last member of staff in the direwolf's enclosure before he is gone." Even saying it was hard. Was she really going to knowingly release a wild creature into the city?

It seemed she was.

"They'll be hunting you as well as him, Sienna, but he can hide in his human form. It will be harder for you."

"I know." She nodded, the image of her zoology certificate being ripped up suddenly flashed before her. But that was only a bit of paper and this was real life. This was a chance to truly help an almost extinct species. "How many of you are there?"

"Not many, numbers are dwindling. We need more babies born. Grady would make a great father."

"Babies? Do you mean wolf pups?"

"No, our children are born as human, they don't shift until they hit puberty."

"Okay, I get it." She blew out a breath. His words had sealed the deal in her head. These were people first and foremost and people did not belong in a zoo. "I'll find somewhere to hide out, lay low, until it blows over. Always fancied Costa Rica to be honest."

"What? Are you crazy?" He turned to her with wide eyes.

"No, the wildlife is great there and—"

"You're coming with us." There was steely determination in his voice.

"With you?"

"Yeah, if you're on the run because you've helped us then you come with us. No one gets left behind. We'll protect you, provide for you, show you our life away from the city."

"Go with you?"

"It's not up for debate." He released her and turned back to the zoo. "You think Ted will be a problem?"

"No, I can handle him, he trusts me implicitly. As

43

does everyone else in the zoo."

Once more she used her security pass to gain entry.

Ted looked up, surprise crossing his features. "You're back?"

"Yeah, I had an idea to shut the grays up. Thought it was worth a try."

"Anything is worth a try." He looked at Tarl. "You better sign in again, buddy."

"Sure thing." Tarl reached for the pen though his attention was on the grainy black-and-white screens on Ted's desk.

"Come on," Sienna said, leading the way.

Soon they were in the canine "staff only" section.

"The grays will stop howling as soon at Grady's scent is gone," Tarl said. "He's encroached on their territory and they're anxious that he'll attack and claim it for himself. Even on his own he could take out most of them, even more so because they're soft captive wolves."

"So that's what it is?" She nodded. "I thought so."

"They're scared, real scared. The fear has been passed down through generations. Direwolves have been known to eat a gray if hungry enough." Tarl reached up and knocked a camera to face the wall.

"What are you doing?"

"Let's just do this quick. We don't want anything on camera if we can help it." He rushed up to the direwolf cage. "Grady, come here."

The direwolf slunk from the shadows looking even thinner than before and his eyes dull.

"I told you to eat!" Tarl said.

The direwolf shook his head and then looked at Sienna.

"She knows everything, and she's going to get you out," Tarl said, dropping his rucksack to the ground.

"And I have clothes for you, so hurry up and shift and we can get the hell away from here."

Still the direwolf did nothing.

"Grady, we have to be quick." Tarl looked at Sienna. "Show him the key."

Quickly Sienna dug into her pocket. "Here. I can open the cage, but only if you're human." Would he shift? Could he shift? Or had Tarl been stringing her along with this crazy story?

But then Grady pushed onto his back legs, and his fur seemed to blur and his limbs lengthened and became flesh colored. The face that emerged was slim and stubbled, his hair jet black.

"Oh, fuck," she muttered. "He really is a man."

"Hurry." Tarl snatched the key from her and unlocked the cage door. He rushed in and scooped Grady close.

Grady clung to Tarl, his eyes closed, his jaw tight. "You came for me."

"Of course. I would never leave you. I'd die with you rather than leave you." He pulled back and stared into Grady's eyes. "I'd never desert you."

"Clothes." Sienna dropped to the rucksack and began pulling out jeans, a sweater, and sneakers. "Get dressed."

Grady was beside her, getting dressed, breathing fast. He was slimmer than Tarl, his muscles less defined, it was clear he'd been starving.

As soon as he was dressed Tarl rushed back the way they'd come, glancing around as he did so. Grady followed, Sienna behind him. She locked her keys away. Her heart was clattering and adrenaline had made her knees a little weak and shaky.

"Wait," she said as they reached Ted's office. "I'll go in first, distract him."

Tarl nodded. Grady was looking around, his eyes darting this way and that, peering into every shadowy corner.

"Hey, Ted, can you hear that?" She stepped in with her hand cupped around her ear.

"What?" He was tapping the screen of the camera Tarl had moved. "Hear what?"

"I think the grays have stopped?"

"Ah, yes, good, but this camera has stopped too. What the heck?" He poked at a few keys on his pad then frowned at the black screen.

Out of the corner of her eye, Sienna saw Tarl and Grady slipping out of the office. For two big guys they were incredibly stealthy.

"Ah, crap, I'll have to go and check it." Ted stood, scraping the legs of his chair. "God knows what's happened to it, pesky squirrel again probably, they jump on them, see, and move them to face the wall."

Sienna didn't hang around. She slipped out of the office and off zoo premises with her entire body buzzing and her mind whirring with the enormity of what she'd just done.

Chapter Five

Tarl and Grady were waiting for her within the darkness of a large overhanging tree.

"Now what?" she asked quietly.

"Your place?" Tarl said. "You'll need a few things to take with you."

"Yeah, lets get the hell out of this city." Grady's voice was deep and rasping. "I hate the damn place." He frowned.

"How will we travel?" Sienna asked, feeling slightly nervous of Grady. He had a wild look about him, his eyes and hair, and he was a fraction taller than Tarl.

"Train," Tarl said. "North."

"I'm never fucking going back to Montana," Grady said, beginning to walk toward the tunnel. "Where the fuck did that ranger come from?"

"No idea." Tarl grabbed Sienna's hand, gave her a reassuring smile, and they caught up with Grady. "But forget that now. We need to look forward, concentrate on getting to Eastern Canada. Keep Sienna safe."

"Why isn't she safe?" Grady threw her a glance as he strode along.

"Man, she just busted you out of the zoo, and keeping animals in the zoo is her main responsibility."

"Fine profession." Grady huffed.

"Hey, you want to go back in there?" Sienna snapped. "Could be arranged."

Tarl squeezed her hand. "He'll come around, it's raw right now."

She pouted into the darkness. "Eastern Canada. Sounds cold."

"Real cold, honey, pack your warmest." Grady

grunted.

After a few minutes she let them into her apartment.

Grady looked around. "You got a bed in here?"

"Yes, behind that curtain." She showed him.

"Any food?" He opened the fridge.

"Er, not really? I tend to eat on the run. But what do you want? Pizza? There's a pizza place at the end of the block, twenty-four seven, I could go get some."

He studied her. "You would do that for me?"

"You haven't eaten for days despite my best efforts, it would be really great to see you eat."

His shoulders relaxed a little and he nodded. "Pizza would be good. Thanks."

"Cool, I'll be back soon. Make yourselves at home." She pointed at the bathroom. "Take a shower if you want."

"Might just do that."

Sienna slipped back out to the street and hurried to Pizza Perfect. She ordered three large, all-meat toppings.

After ten minutes she was paying and stacking the warm boxes on top of each other. "Thanks."

"You're real hungry, Doll." The pizza guy raised his eyebrows. "Or are you having a late-night party?"

"Something like that."

She hurried back to her apartment. The less people who saw her the better. Her face would probably be all over the news in twenty-four hours and everyone on her block would be questioned by NYPD.

With the scent of oregano, cheese, and spice wafting upward she let herself back into her home. After setting down the pizza, she paused and listened. The small living area was empty but the shower was running.

The bathroom door was slightly open, and both

Tarl and Grady were in there together.

Her breath hitched as she peeked in. They were naked, their big wet bodies filling her shower cubicle. Grady was standing facing the wall and Tarl was soaping his back. He was doing a thorough job and as Sienna took in the whole scene, she saw he had an erection.

Her pussy fluttered as a pleasant memory of showering with him the night before blustered into her mind. He'd been damn good at pinning her against that very wall and driving them both to orgasm. Hell, yeah.

Grady turned around and stared at Tarl. He was older, she could see that now, he had none of Tarl's youthful roundness to his jawline or shoulders, he was more rugged, sharper, darker. He was a beautiful man, that couldn't be denied.

Without saying a word Grady took Tarl's hand in his. He set it on his own chest and trailed it downward, over his wet skin, taut abs, and to his stiff cock. "Do it."

Sienna had only just heard the instruction but her breath became shallow. She should step away, stop watching, she knew that. She didn't. It was as if something magnetic was holding her there.

It was more than curiosity, more than the erotic scene, it was also part indignation. If Tarl and Grady were an item, what had last night meant between her and Tarl? He'd acted as though he were young, free, and single for goodness sake.

Tarl took Grady's big cock in his hand.

Grady closed his eyes and tipped his head back so his crown rested on the wall. Water sluiced over his chin, his neck, and down his tense body.

Tarl began to jerk him off. Firm, steady movements as though he knew from practice just how Grady liked it.

"Fuck, yeah," Grady grunted, his fists clenching

at his sides. "That's it, but be quick."

Tarl sped up, watching Grady's face closely as he worked him.

Grady locked his knees. Each time Tarl rubbed him to the root, the tip of his cock protruded from Tarl's fist. It was very domed with a thickly flared glans.

Sienna felt her nipples tingle as a shot of desire went through her body. Damn, Grady had been impressive as a direwolf but he was incredible as a man. She rubbed her fingers over her palms wondering what his hard cock would feel like at this moment, just before he came.

"Fuck…" Grady gasped. "Yeah … more…"

Tarl didn't reply, he was also breathing fast, his breath hitching and his teeth gritted.

"Ah! Yeah." Grady snapped his hand out and gripped Tarl's shoulder. "Fuck…"

Pearly fluid burst from his cock and instantly became washed away by the stream of water.

"Fuck … I needed that." Grady was gasping for breath as he continued to come. His entire body trembled and he let out a long groan.

And then he reached for Tarl, dragged him close, and set his mouth over his in a ravenous kiss.

Sienna stepped back and swallowed, her mouth dry. She shouldn't have seen that. But hell, they were in her shower and hadn't closed the bathroom door. This was her place.

She turned and dropped her keys in a ceramic bowl. "I'm home. I've got pizza," she called loudly and probably overly jovial.

The shower went off, and by the time she'd reached the refrigerator and poured a glass of wine, Tarl was behind her with a white towel wrapped around his waist. It did nothing to cover the fact he still had an erection.

"Smells incredible," he said.

"Yeah, they're pretty reliable down there." She avoided staring at his groin or glancing in the direction of the bathroom. "Want a beer?"

"Sure, thanks. Grady will have one too."

She didn't reply and set the drinks on the table before lifting the lid on a pepperoni and taking a slice.

Tarl turned his back to her and dropped the towel.

As she bit into melty cheese she admired his high tight ass cheeks with little dimples on the sides. He pulled on sweats and turned to her with a knowing glint in his eyes.

He knew she'd ogled him. But thank goodness he didn't know she'd watched him jerking off Grady.

A needle of irritation poked her again. How could he have flirted, seduced her, made love to her when he was in a relationship? Because he clearly was. Why else would he have been prepared to take such risks to save Grady?

Grady wandered into the room fully dressed and scrubbing his wet hair with a small blue towel. "Looks good. What do we owe you?"

"Nothing." She shrugged and carried on eating.

A siren wailed on the street outside.

"Looking for me?" Grady said as he held both beer and pizza.

"If Ted has spotted you're missing, then maybe." The pizza suddenly seemed heavy on its way to her stomach. "But he probably won't have, he'll presume you're sleeping in the shadows. It will be morning before the alarm goes out."

"And we need to be gone." Tarl frowned. "What time is the first train north? We should get to the border as soon as possible."

Sienna set down her pizza and reached for her phone.

"We can go from Penn to Montreal in the morning, six a.m."

"That'll do but I don't want you going through any border control," Tarl said.

"Why not?"

"Honey." Grady leaned forward with a new softness to his face. "You need to be untraceable. You're a fugitive now, they just don't know it yet."

She gulped.

"So we'll get off near the border and run." Tarl nodded.

"Run." She downturned her mouth. "Not really my thing."

"No, but it's ours." Grady bit into his pizza. "And I'm sure you'll enjoy riding us."

"Riding you?" She looked between them.

Tarl chuckled as he continued to demolish pizza.

"And do they do private rooms on the train?" Grady said nodding at the phone. "The less people see you, the better."

Sienna looked at the screen. "Yes, first-class bedroom, it's expensive."

"Book it, money is no object," Grady said. "We'll pay you back."

"How can money be no object? Money is always relevant."

"We've inherited over the years," Tarl said. "Ancestors who've been good with money, invested, worked hard. We don't need it really, wolves don't, no animal does. It's a human concept and since we are only half human we don't think about it until a moment like this and then we find we have plenty."

"Oh, I see." She paused. "And where we're going,

we don't need money?"

"Not much, a few groceries for the humans, the odd medical bill. But if we're hungry, we go out and hunt. If our cabin leaks, we sleep in the forest. Do you see where I'm coming from?" Grady leaned forward studying her.

"Yes, I think so." She bit on her bottom lip.

He watched her intently.

"And so," she asked, questions mounting in her mind. "Where we're going, this place with cabins, there are other humans there, not just direwolves?"

"We're going to Kochi and I think you'll like it. And yes, some of the direwolves have mated with humans, bred with them. Soon you'll meet them all."

"Our babies are stronger if they are half shifter and half human," Tarl said. "It's preferable, in fact, and we do everything that is preferable to continue the species. It's a priority."

"Interesting." She nodded, the scientist in her storing away this fact about babies with a plan to delve deeper at some point. "But won't these humans turn me in to the authorities? There's bound to be a bounty on my head, a reward."

"What? No!" Tarl said loudly. "We're a pack, we look out for each other. They would never turn you in, once you're part of the pack you'll be protected at all costs. Nothing will change that."

"Loyalty is unwavering," Grady went on. "When I've spoken, ordered something, it will happen without dispute, and they will all know from the beginning that you are a very special woman, Sienna, that you have risked everything for direwolves. You will be safe, I promise you that with everything I am."

She nodded and felt reassured. It certainly sounded like a fascinating social structure to be part of. It was also clear that Grady was alpha male, or considered himself to be. The gray wolves had an alpha male who dominated the group and held top position with fierce determination.

"The bedroom, on the train." Tarl nodded at the phone.

"Oh, yes, I'll do that now." She booked the room for three. One way. "We need to be out at first light, in fact before that."

"What time does the security at the zoo change shift?" Tarl asked.

"Seven."

"Then we leave at five. Get to the station and board the moment we can." He nodded at her floor-to-ceiling cupboard. "Pack warm and pack anything that can't be replaced, but remember you'll have to carry it in a rucksack."

She nodded and racked her brain. She'd take the jewelry her adoptive mother had left her and some photographs from childhood. There was a *Zoology* magazine she'd had a report published in, that was precious, but other than that there wasn't much. She didn't hold sentiment to inanimate objects, she was more interested in the living.

Grady rubbed his belly and let out a sigh. "That pizza was good. Thanks." He nodded at the bedroom area with the curtain hanging in front of it. "You mind if I lie down? Haven't been sleeping so well."

"Go for it," she said. "I have to pack."

"Yeah, I'll help Sienna," Tarl said. "Get some sleep, Grady, you need to recover from your starvation."

"That was self-inflicted, I might add." Sienna raised her eyebrows at him. "You had top quality chicken and beef you could have eaten."

"And break a direwolf oath?" Grady stood and

huffed. "Never." He wandered to the curtain, looking far too big for her small apartment, and pushed the curtain back. The bed creaked when he dropped onto it.

Sienna set about organizing a rucksack to take what would be her worldly possessions in her new life.

Tarl cleared away the pizza boxes and bottles then stood at the window peering into the darkness.

A while later Grady's steady, slightly rough breathing could be heard. He was sleeping soundly.

"He always sleeps better if he knows I'm awake," Tarl said as looked out the window.

Sienna put her bag by the door. She didn't reply.

"And he needs this rest before we travel," Tarl added.

She studied his long back, his long legs, and the way he held himself as though ready to spring into action, attack or defend. He was a man of strength and beauty, yet he'd deceived her.

"What's wrong?" he said, suddenly turning.

She scowled, how had he known her irritation was rising?

"Tell me." He didn't move from the window.

So she went and stood next to him, stared out at the Empire State Building, which was lit up with the image of a wolf as a nod to the direwolf being in New York City.

"You had me believe you were single," she said quietly, even though the words were big. "You lied to me."

"What?"

"It's clear you and Grady are an item."

"Sienna, it's not what you think … really."

VOLUME ONE

Chapter Six

"So, what is it like?" Sienna asked. "Between you and Grady?"

"He's an alpha, my alpha, and he's also…"

"What?"

"You saw us, didn't you?"

"I don't know what you mean?"

"In the shower."

She pressed her lips into a tight line and looked down at her feet.

He cupped his hand over his left ear and leaned closer to her. "I have very acute hearing, even as a human it's pretty awesome compared to yours. I heard you come in. I heard your breath hitch when I took Grady's cock in my hand. Hell, at one point I thought I could hear your heart beating, fast, when he came."

Sienna felt her cheeks heat. "So why didn't you stop? Shut the door, tell me to fuck off?" She folded her arms over her chest and glared up at him.

"Because I didn't mind, and Grady wouldn't care. He just wanted to release some tension."

"And you were the man for the job."

"Sienna." He reached for her but she stepped away. "Please," he said. "I can explain."

"I'm not stupid. You're a couple, hell, you even finish each other's sentences."

Tarl ran his hand through his hair and narrowed his eyes. "Okay, we are a couple, a committed couple, but that doesn't mean I cheated on him with you, and it doesn't mean I—we—don't have room for you in our lives." He paused. "You're not just beautiful and intelligent and kind, you've done something for us direwolves that is so selfless. Of course we're drawn to you, of course we want you."

He reached for her again and this time she let his hands rest on her shoulders.

"Sienna, you are part of the pack now, part of us. There is no changing that."

"Part of the pack?"

"Yes." He leaned closer and pressed his forehead on hers.

The scent of shower gel filled her nose and his breath was warm on her lips. She felt surrounded by his strength and conviction and for a moment the serious situation she was in almost faded away. She wasn't alone.

"I still want you," he said. "If we didn't have to leave soon, I'd be stripping you naked and making us both come until we're exhausted."

"Tarl," she managed. "But...?"

"And Grady would watch, hell, no, he'd join in. He wouldn't be able to resist you."

She stared into his eyes. She'd never had a threesome but that certainly sounded what Tarl was suggesting could happen.

"When we're at Kochi," he murmured then brushed his lips over hers. "You'll see how it can be between the three of us."

"The three of us?" In the name of the Lord, when she'd hooked up with Tarl the night before, she thought it would be for a night of fun with a sexy twenty-something, she never could have predicted he'd be talking about their life together.

Their life with Grady! In Canada. Living with a pack of direwolves.

She let out a sigh. "This is all so much to get my head around."

"I know." He slipped his arms from her shoulders

and around her body, pulling her close. "It is for us too. One minute we were in Montana, then New York, and now the secret of our existence is out. And now … now we've met you, now we are more than two."

Sienna slid her arms around him and held him tight, the way he was holding her. There was something about him that made her feel like she could be completely herself, show her fears and hopes.

"Your family will miss you. Your friends," he murmured. "They'll be shocked."

"I don't have much family, a few distant aunts and uncles, that's it. I was adopted, my adoptive parents died a few years ago, both of cancer."

"I'm sorry." He stroked her hair. "That's rough."

She swallowed and closed her eyes. "Yes, it was, they were my parents, I never even thought of the ones who gave me up."

He was quiet for a moment. "Friends?"

"My friends are at the zoo, I am—was—a bit of an all-work-and-no-play kind of girl. And now when they find out I released a dangerous predator into the city, they'll hate me."

At that moment Grady let out a particularly loud snore.

Sienna looked his way and giggled. "Dangerous predator?"

Tarl also laughed quietly. "As the saying goes, let sleeping dogs lie."

****

A few hours later Sienna locked her apartment door for what she believed would be the last time. The most likely scenario was in a few hours the NYPD would be knocking on it, looking for her, the most wanted zookeeper of all time.

"Come on," Grady said, looking up at the sky. "The sun will be rising soon."

Tarl hitched his rucksack on and then checked a strap on Sienna's. "You okay?"

"I've got to be." She gave him a half smile.

"You're gonna be great." He took her hand. "And if you wobble, we've got you."

Soon they were hurrying toward Penn Station. It was a lengthy walk but it had been decided it was best to keep Sienna's identity as low-key as possible.

When they finally got there, she pulled down her cap as the tickets were checked and then averted her face from a few other passengers as they made their way to their sleeper carriage.

"This should do," Tarl said, stepping in and shucking off his rucksack into a corner.

"It's cozy," Sienna said, looking at the small space that really was just a bed and a tiny table. There was a note on the bed saying to ring the bell to have it turned into two sofas.

Grady looked left and right along the corridor then stepped in and shut the door, clicked the lock. He checked a door to his right. "Ah, a tiny bathroom, well, a toilet and sink at least."

"That's good." Tarl nodded. "It means we can keep Sienna hidden right to the border."

She sighed, removed her cap and winter coat, then sat on the bed, which was softer than she'd anticipated. "I am quite tired." She hadn't slept all night.

"Then close your eyes," Tarl said. "I'm going to go to the canteen carriage as soon as this thing starts moving. Get us some food."

She kicked off her boots and lay down.

Grady pulled the curtain so anyone walking on the

platform wouldn't see in.

Her phone buzzed from her coat pocket.

"What's that?" Grady asked.

"A message?"

"Should we look?" Tarl pulled it out.

Sienna supressed a yawn and took it. "It's from Bethany."

"Who is Bethany?"

"She is a junior member of staff on the canine team." As she'd spoken her mouth dried and she opened the message: **What the hell? The direwolf is gone and they are saying you were the last one with him. Everyone is going mad around here. Call me. Call someone.**

Her heart skipped a beat. "Oh, fuck."

"What?" Tarl asked.

"It's started. They know you're gone." She looked at Grady and passed him the phone.

His jaw tensed and his eyes flashed. "We knew they'd discover my disappearance at some point. We have to be grateful we got this far. The chances of them looking here before we pull out of the station are slim."

"Let's hope so." She squeezed the bridge of her nose.

"They'll be searching the park, then going to your place," Tarl said. He glanced at a round brass clock on the wall. "And we'll be on our way in ten minutes with luck."

Her phone buzzed again, then again. More messages, all work colleagues.

She turned it facedown on the bed. Then it started to ring. She glanced at the number, not one she recognized, and then ended the call.

"Turn it off," Grady said. "Can't they trace you with those things?"

"Fuck, you're right, I think they might be able to." Quickly she turned her phone off. The dark screen was better than the flashing and buzzing.

"Want me to get rid of it?" Tarl asked.

"Er, no, not for now."

"But…"

"It's got photographs on it, of animals I've cared for, studied … I have sentimental attachment to them."

"But you can't look at them if you have your phone off."

"I know, but I also can't throw them away."

"Fair enough." Tarl shrugged and sat on one of the small chairs that had been stowed under the table.

Sienna lay back down and rested her forearm over her eyes. She was a fugitive, a runaway, a criminal, not descriptions she would have ever labeled herself with, but it was the truth. And it was a truth she was happy with … sort of. Ultimately, she'd saved a direwolf from starving to death, saved a life, and that was the bottom line.

Soon the train began to move, slowly at first, the clunk of the tracks a lazy sound beneath her, but as they got out of the city and the golden glow of dawn lit their cabin, it sped up.

She'd slept for some time, feeling watched over and safe, and when she woke there was a scattering of food wrappers on the table. Tarl had obviously been true to his word and gone in search of sustenance.

"Hey, sleepyhead," he said, crawling onto the bed next to her. "Feeling better?"

"Yes, how long was I out for?"

"About three hours."

"Or one hundred and sixty miles from New York, depending on which way you look at it." Grady stood from where he'd been hunched on a small chair and stretched, his fingers touching the ceiling of their cabin.

He dropped his arms with a sigh. "Always good to put distance between yourself and the hunters."

"I couldn't agree more." She smiled up at Tarl whose face was hovering over hers. "How are you feeling?"

"I'm all good, I have a full stomach and Grady and you with me, I need little else in this world."

The truth in his eyes had her heart swelling and she touched his stubbled cheek. "Is it really that simple for you?"

"You better believe it." He set his mouth over hers and kissed her.

It was a lovely lazy kiss that combined with the rocking of the train was almost hypnotic. She sighed into it and ran her fingers through his thick strands of hair.

As he leaned closer, his body heat radiating onto hers, a shot of lust went into her bloodstream. Tarl was sexy, and he felt and smelled amazing. She wanted him closer, closer still, and she arched up so their chests connected.

"Fuck, you're sexy," he murmured then kissed over her cheek to her ear.

"So are you." She smiled and closed her eyes as he dipped his hand to her waist and then ran it over the curve of her hip, over her pants.

"I think you both are sexy as fuck."

The bed sank a little as Grady crawled onto it and settled on her opposite side.

"You ever had a threesome?" he whispered against her ear.

"No." A kernel of excitement popped in her stomach.

"So, you haven't been fucked by two guys, one after the other, or at the same time?"

"No."

"She's not ready for that," Tarl said stiffly.

"You don't call the shots." Grady frowned at him.

"I know her better than you." Tarl stroked the back of his thumb down her cheek then traced her lips. He stared into her eyes. "Not yet, she's not ready for you, Grady."

Grady made a huffing sound and then cupped her cheek and turned her to face him. "My beta might be right so we can wait, but it will happen." His eyes were like chips of ice off a glacier.

"Don't I get a choice?"

"Sure, honey, but I know you'll want it." He chuckled and instantly the darkness went from him. "You'll be begging for it, the way Tarl does."

"I can't deny that," Tarl said, undoing the zipper on her hoodie. "Or that I want you naked, now."

"Naked?"

"We've got time to pass, and I can see desire in your eyes, Sienna, hell, I can smell it coming off you." He breathed deep and closed his eyes.

"You cannot."

He twitched his eyebrows and set to work undoing the buttons on her pants. "Do you want to me to make you come again? You know I'm good for it."

For a moment she was lulled by the sound of the train on the tracks and then she nodded. She was surrounded by hot, hard, horny men, an orgasm seemed like the best plan, not least in case the police boarded and she was arrested and spent the rest of her life wearing orange.

"Hey, don't worry about anything, we're here." Grady's voice was softer as he reached down to remove her pants.

She pushed thoughts of a train raid from her mind and suddenly realized she was utterly naked. The guys were still fully clothed.

"How did…?"

"So fucking sexy…" Grady blew out a breath and took her right nipple between his thumb and index finger and tweaked and tugged. "Been years since I was with a woman … and I don't think ever one as sweet and delicate as you."

Her belly quivered and she curled her toes. What he was doing to her nipple was on the point of discomfort but the sensation went straight to her pussy and her clit was twitching with need.

"You ready to be adored?" Tarl asked against her lips.

She nodded.

He smiled at her then ducked his head to kiss her neck, peppering her flesh with hot caresses of his lips.

Grady switched his attention to her other nipple then tipped forward and kissed her on the lips. Unlike Tarl there was no gentle probing. He was kissing her and he took full control. She gave herself up to it, to him, and gripped the ball of his solid shoulder.

"You taste of a spring day in the forest," he said, breaking the kiss and brushing a strand of hair from her face. "Beautiful."

Before she could answer he was kissing her again and his palm roaming over her chest, exploring the shape of her breasts.

Tarl's touch dipped lower. He circled her navel and then fluffed his fingertips through her small patch of pubic hair.

She canted her hips, wanting to feel more, needing to start a climb to the orgasm he'd promised. She was so turned on. Having two sexy guys worshiping her body was even better than she'd imagined.

"Are you wet?" Tarl whispered into her ear.

"Have we made you wet for us yet?"

"I want you," she said, parting her legs until they butted up with theirs. "I want you to touch me … there."

"What, here?" Tarl said, stroking over her clit with a firm touch.

"Oh! Yes, there." She curled her toes and fisted his sweater. "Please, Tarl."

"You don't have to say please, we're going to give you what you need," Grady said pulling back a fraction to look down at her body. "We're always going to give you everything you need."

She nodded and watched as Grady trailed his finger over her flat stomach, over her pubic hair, and then overtook Tarl's finger on her clit. He then slid through her damp folds and found her entrance.

"This where you need me?" he asked in a maddeningly calm voice.

She nodded and her breath hitched.

He smiled, just a little, a tilt of the right side of his mouth. And then he pushed into her entrance with two big fingers.

She moaned and arched her back, pressing down onto him.

Tarl circled her clit with the pads of his fingers, a slow firm caress that instantly had a pressure beginning to build.

"So fucking responsive," Tarl murmured. "Hell, yeah."

Sienna canted her hips, lost to the feel of their hands on her. She lifted her head and looked down between her legs. Two large male hands working her, hair-coated forearms with tendons taut, her skin pale and delicate in comparison. "Oh, fuck…" she gasped, the erotic sight imprinting itself on her brain. "Fuck, yes."

"Come like this," Grady said and added another

finger to the two he was already fucking her with. "Come for us."

The new denser, thicker invasion had her body turning to steel and getting ready to explode. Tarl sped up, the stimulation on her clit fast and resolute. He would not stop until she came, that was a certain.

"Squirt for us, show Grady how you come," Tarl said.

"Oh, fuck, I don't know … I don't want…" The gush that wet her thighs and the bed when she'd come before was embarrassing.

"Don't say you don't want to, it's fucking awesome," Tarl said. "So damn satisfying for me to know you're experiencing such pleasure."

"But…"

"No buts … squirt," Grady said. "Or we'll keep making you come until you do."

"As threats go, that's not … very … compelling," she managed. The pressure was reaching tipping point. There was so much pleasure stored up in her, and it was about to release in an almighty climax.

She held her breath, gripped both Tarl and Grady, and forced her eyes to stay open, watching their hands on her, their fingers driving her to the most wonderful type of insanity.

"Yes, yes, come…" Tarl said.

A flush of red rushed up her chest and prickled her cheeks. Her heart clattered against her sternum and then she let it release—a huge rush of ecstasy that had her crying out and bucking from the bed.

They stayed with her, the wet sounds of flesh on flesh clicking around the room. Soft heat, wetness, basted her thighs, she'd squirted again, the release of fluid adding to her pleasure.

"Fuck, that's hot." Grady stared down at her. "My

hand is soaked, you just flooded it."

"I … I…" She was struggling for breath. Her pussy was clamping and releasing around his fingers. Over and over. Each spasm a new wave of bliss that fluttered its way around her body.

"God, yeah." Tarl captured her mouth and kissed her, his breaths coming fast too. "You did it again."

Sienna had no idea why this had started happening to her, though the orgasms Tarl had given her, and now this one, were very intense, very powerful. Perhaps that was the difference to her previous nothing-to-write-home-about lovers.

"When we fuck it will feel even better," Grady said against her temple. "You'll forget what damn planet you live on."

Chapter Seven

Sienna lay on a fresh sheet in a lazy naked slumber after her intense orgasm at the hands of two men. She tossed words like "fugitive" and "criminal" from her thoughts and lay wrapped in Grady's embrace.

He was holding her as though seeing her afresh, feeling something new in her. He'd mellowed since his anxiety levels about being captured had eased but this was new again, now he was positively doting.

He stroked her hair, kissed her cheek, and wound his legs with hers. He'd removed his sweater and she was enjoying having her palm flat on his warm hair-coated chest.

"Do you think he'll be long?" she murmured.

"Tarl? Nah, he'll soon find some information about what's going on in New York. Hopefully the search hasn't stretched beyond the city."

"Perhaps not for you, but maybe for me?" She paused. "Do you think they'll presume we're together?"

"They'd be right." He raised her hand and kissed her knuckles. "Yesterday you had me under lock and key, right now I feel like you're taking possession of a different part of me."

"What do you mean?"

He twisted is lips as though thinking of his answer. "I'm half direwolf, half human, the same as Tarl, so you have to understand that our thought processes and emotions are different from yours. We have a different biology."

"Go on."

"I guess what I'm trying to say is we fall in love hard and fast. When we know someone is right for us, when we want that person, or direwolf, at our side, the decision is made. It doesn't waver, we're decisive, and that's for practical reasons. The wilderness is a tough place, why make it tougher?"

"You fall in love hard and fast?" she repeated.

"Yes, and it's pretty obvious to me that Tarl is already in love with you."

"He is not."

"I know him better than anyone, and I see it in his eyes when he looks at you, the way his attention follows you around a room, how he knew in his heart you could help us, even if he didn't understand the future at that point."

She was quiet for a moment and watched the flashing light in the window as the train passed through trees. "I like him, a lot. I trust him, something I haven't been too good at in the past."

"Trust is vital to any relationship."

"I agree." She stroked from his sternum to his nipple and traced a circle around it, disturbing the hairs. "How long have you been together?"

"We had an attraction as soon as he started shifting, but I made him wait, it seemed the right thing to do."

"Because you're older than him?"

"Yeah. I gotta set an example to the pack. I'm alpha, remember."

"I remember." She studied his face. "How much older are you?"

"He's twenty-two, I'm forty. And you?"

"I'm thirty-five."

"I guess Tarl has a type then—older." He laughed softly, his chest rising and falling.

"Can I ask you something personal?"

"Sure."

"Do you … you know … fuck, when you're direwolves, when you've shifted?"

"No, we don't. Some do, not our thing."

"Oh, I see." She found herself glad about that. "Why isn't it your thing?"

"It doesn't seem as intimate somehow. When I fuck Tarl, I like to see his face, feel his flesh, not fur, I want to hear his words not howls."

She nodded and tried to imagine them fucking. Perhaps she wouldn't have to, maybe they'd let her watch when they eventually got to Kochi.

There was a knock at the door.

Grady got up, his movements swift and efficient. "Tarl?"

"Yeah, let me in."

Quickly Grady opened the door. "Heard anything?"

"Yeah, everyone's phones are blowing up with it."

"What are they saying?" Sienna pushed to sitting and then proceeded to dress.

"Residents of New York have been told to stay indoors because of a dangerous beast on the loose."

Grady shrugged. "Good advice. If I hadn't had that pizza I'd be damn hungry."

Tarl held up his hand, his expression serious. "Your face is everywhere, Sienna. Not that we should be surprised."

"Everywhere?"

"Yeah, it's a good thing we've got this private cabin. Ten minutes out there and you'd be recognized."

She slapped on her baseball cap, went to the window, and stared out at the passing wilderness. "So, what are we going to do?" She fought down a rise of fear. Her image was everywhere. The entire nation was looking for her. She was the "wanted" person who'd released the dangerous direwolf.

Grady picked up a packet of crisps and opened them. He sat back, one ankle crossed over the other knee, and began to eat.

"I suggest we get off at the next stop," Tarl said and pulled a leaflet from his pocket. "We've made good progress and it's a small town, we could run north and be over the border in an hour from there."

"Gosh, we have made good progress," Sienna said.

"In all truth, you've been either asleep or writhing in ecstasy." Grady raised his eyebrows at her.

"Best way to be." She grinned, even though anxiety was rapidly knotting in her stomach.

"How long until our next stop?" Grady asked.

"Twenty minutes. We'll wait until the last minute to get off and just make a dash for it."

"Yeah, and if Sienna keeps her head down, cap on, hood up, shielded by us, hopefully no one will spot her."

"Do you think that will work?" she asked.

"It's the best plan we have." Tarl set his hand on her shoulder. "Make sure you've had a snack and are ready to go. But remember, we've got your back, it will be okay."

"We'll make damn sure it is." Grady crumpled up his crisp packet and tossed it into the trash. "Our lives depend upon it."

As the train slowed and then came to a halt, Sienna stiffened with anticipation. They had to pass through an entire carriage of people to get to the nearest exit. Tarl had done a check, and she'd need to go quick, head down, just in case anyone saw that she was America's most wanted woman and raised the alarm.

"Stay close to me," Grady said, stepping in front of her. "Hold my sweater, here." He tugged the hem that sat over the rise of his ass. "That way you won't have to look where you're going. I'll guide you."

"And I'll be right behind, so don't stop," Tarl said.

She reached out and steadied herself as the train came to a complete halt. The absence of noise, the wheels clacking on the rails, was suddenly loud.

"Just keep walking," Grady said. "Let's go."

She did as he'd instructed, following tucked in behind him, she spotted passengers in her peripheral vision. They were reading books, looking at phones, chatting. As each one passed, she felt a little safer. Nearly there.

Then, just as they were about to step off, a shout came their way. "Hey, you there! Wait."

Her heart stuttered and she scooted closer to Grady. He didn't stop, he alighted the train then turned and took her into the curve of his arm.

She'd lost Tarl's presence behind her.

"What's going on?" she asked, fear sliding into her veins. Was this it? Was this as far as she was going to get?"

"Your scarf, sir, you've dropped it."

"It's okay," Grady said, "Tarl dropped something, it's only the guard."

"Is he looking at me?"

"No, and we won't give him a chance." Grady walked to the right, heading along the platform at speed. "Tarl will catch us up."

Sure enough, by the time they'd ducked out of the station and navigated past a row of cabs, Tarl was beside them again. "Damn scarf," he muttered. "Didn't even realize it had come out of my rucksack."

Grady shrugged. "We'll go north."

"How?" Sienna risked a look around.

The town was quiet, not a tourist spot, and there had been a frost making the ground sparkle.

"I told you, you can ride." Tarl grinned and winked.

"I'm not sure if—"

"Not really any choice, honey." Grady shrugged. "But we can't shift here, we need to get to the forest. This way."

He didn't wait for the others to agree and headed off, Sienna still in the safety of his arm.

A car drove past, stuttering from its exhaust, and two children pedaled frantically in a race with each other to a chilly looking park. A ginger cat stepped in front of them and instantly hissed, arching as it backed away.

"Cats hate us," Tarl said. "Whether we're human or direwolves."

"They've never liked me either," Sienna said. "I guess that's why I ended up working in the canine enclosure."

After ten minutes of walking, they came to the last of the houses. Before them stretched a dense-looking forest. A slight mist hung over the tips of the fir trees and a huge bird of prey soared in the heavy gray sky.

"Come on," Grady sped up, as though the need to shift was getting greater. "We're almost there."

"And then what? You shift and I just climb onboard?"

"And hold on tight." Tarl curled his hand over her shoulder.

"How long for?"

"It will take us an hour to cross the border then we'll go northeast for another three hours. That should get us there late evening."

"To Kochi?"

"Yeah, to Kochi."

She nodded. Was she strong enough to hold onto the back of a direwolf for so long? She hoped so, and there was only one way to find out.

The hard ground crunched underfoot and the air was damp and heavy with the scent of mulch.

Tarl dropped his rucksack to the ground and began to strip off.

Grady was still searching, looking for anyone who might spot them shifting.

Sienna knotted her fingers together. She'd seen them both shift now, but would she ever get used to the wonder of it? It really was an incredible thing to witness.

"Come on." Tarl shoved his clothing into the rucksack. "Hand me your stuff."

Grady frowned at him. "Can't be too careful."

Sienna scanned the area behind them. It was a flat field and in the very distance there were a few roofs, one had smoke trickling from a chimney. "I can't see anyone."

"We're in the clear." Tarl clenched and unclenched his fists then rolled his neck.

"Yeah, you're right." Grady pursed his lips as though still anxious. "We've gotta get going."

"Who should I ride?" Sienna pulled her coat zipper right up to her chin.

"I'll take you," Tarl said. "Grady can lead the way, his sense of direction is second to none."

Grady nodded once then shoved his clothes into the rucksack.

Both men were gloriously naked in the forest, their bodies sleek with the damp air and tiny droplets of sparkle sitting in their body hair.

"Don't be afraid of us, we'd never hurt you," Tarl

said.

"I'm not."

"Good." He stretched up, his limbs thickening and his skin hazing as though she'd squinted her eyes. The next thing she knew he was falling to all fours as a direwolf. His nose had elongated, his ears were pricked up, and his body was covered in thick white fur with brown patches. He stepped up to her and nudged her hand with his wet nose.

"Tarl," she whispered stroking the patch between his ears. "You're beautiful." And she meant it, he was utterly stunning.

He half closed his eyes and tipped his head. A low murmur rumbled from his throat.

Grady laughed. "Oh, you just found his sweet spot, we'll be going nowhere if you keep tickling him there."

She tickled him some more then stepped to his side.

He dropped a little, bending his front legs, and she scrabbled onto his back and took hold of two big handfuls of fur. He was wide, at least as wide as a horse she'd used to ride when growing up, and she was just as high from the ground.

"You hold on tight, especially if you see anything he has to jump as he's running." Grady pointed at her. "Promise."

"Yes, promise." She nodded and beat down a wave of anxiety. Her life had gone from crazy busy to just plain crazy. But what choice did she have other than to go with it?

Grady took a deep breath then repeated the same action as Tarl. He rose up onto his toes, stretched, and then fell forward.

This time Sienna tried harder to watch each bit of

his body shift, but it was as though he were shrouded in mist as it happened, and it wasn't until he was a dark direwolf that she could see him clearly again.

He raised his head and let out a long, low howl.

The sound vibrated right into her chest and stirred an emotion she couldn't name. It was primitive and downright evocative.

And then Grady turned, snapped up the rucksack between his jaws, and took off into the darkness. Tarl followed and she ducked to avoid branches then braced as he jumped a log.

Instantly she loved it. He was easy to ride. She didn't feel unstable because their bodies moved as one. The wind whipped moisture from her eyes, and she dashed at it when they raced over a clearing. Beneath them twigs cracked and snapped, and the cool air blasted around her ears noisily.

Grady was charging ahead. Hot breath puffed from his mouth and his powerful legs took great strides. Tarl kept up easily, slipping this way and that around tree trunks. Eventually the forest came to an end and a huge expanse of grazing land stretched before them.

A herd of black cattle spotted them and raised their heads. One decided to run away and the others followed until they were over a ridge and out of sight. Tarl and Grady paid them no notice and kept going.

Sienna had no idea when they'd crossed the border, it could have been any number of places, all unmanned, no roads, just wilderness. They hadn't seen so much as a mounted officer, and it was clear Grady knew how to avoid humans … mostly.

Eventually they came to a halt beside a river. Sienna slid off Tarl and blew into her hands. It was cold. Both Tarl and Grady went to the water and drank deeply.

Sienna pulled a bottle of water from her rucksack

and took a few sips. She also munched on a cereal bar— that would have to do as dinner. It was getting dark. Soon the sun would touch the horizon and slip away.

She looked around, hands on hips, and blew out a breath. At least no one would find her here. She hoped Kochi would feel just as remote and safe. Oh, and a fire would be good too. She didn't have as much fur as her companions.

Chapter Eight

The moon had risen like a giant pearl by the time they reached their destination. Stars had come out to join it and they looked as though salt crystals had been thrown into the air.

Tarl stopped. He was breathing hard, the last hour had been uphill and rough terrain.

Seeing rooftops and the curls of chimney smoke, Sienna slipped from him, landing on the hard ground.

Grady dropped the rucksack, looked at her, the village, and then shifted back to his human form within a matter of seconds. Tarl did the same. He too was breathing hard, and when he shifted his cheeks were red.

"Are you okay, Grady?" Sienna asked.

"Never better, didn't think I'd see this place again." He reached for his pants. "Didn't think I'd see my pack again."

"You better hope you haven't been usurped," Tarl said, also getting dressed quickly.

Grady let out a growling noise. "If Dresdon has done one thing to disrespect me I'll…"

"You'll put him in his place," Tarl said, setting his hand on Grady's shoulder. "And I'll help you."

Grady pulled in a deep breath, nodded, and then put on his boots, lacing them quickly.

"Stick with us," Tarl said, linking his warm hand with Sienna's cold one. "And don't worry, snapping and snarling is usual."

"Snapping and snarling?"

They walked the last hundred meters to Kochi and when they arrived saw that half a dozen people were sitting around a large fire in the center of the cabins.

"Grady! Tarl!" A young woman with long brown

hair leapt to her feet and pointed. "I knew you were coming. I knew we hadn't lost you. I could feel it."

The rest of the group stood, there were gasps and whoops and then they were surrounded.

Everyone wanted to hug Tarl and slap Grady on the back. There were a hundred questions at once and lots of curious glances at Sienna.

A wave of shyness came over her. She was used to being in control and even the center of attention when giving lectures at the zoo, but this was different. This was stepping into a world she had no understanding of. She was the outsider.

But Tarl didn't let go of her hand and when the noise of the chatter calmed, he led her toward the fire that had a huge pot of stew sitting over it.

Suddenly a huge guy, big black beard and shoulders as broad as a mountain, stomped down from one of the cabins. He was glaring at Grady as though he hated him.

"Oh, fuck," Tarl muttered and steered Sienna to a log.

"Who is that?" she asked.

"Dresdon. Sit here, wait." He nodded at the girl with the long brown hair, Billie. "Look after her, Billie."

"Sure." Billie squeezed closer to Sienna. "I can do that."

But Sienna wasn't taking much notice. The huge guy, Dresdon, had marched straight up to Grady with malignant intent in every pace.

Tarl was behind Grady in an instant, as were several other men and women.

Dresdon stood alone. He tipped his chin. "Huh, he's back and you're around him like puppies. Who has led you these last weeks?" He stabbed his thumb against his chest. "Me."

"I'm grateful for you holding the fort," Grady said, folding his arms. "But as you said, I am back now, and last time I looked I was alpha around here."

Dresdon bared his teeth and a strange growling sound came from his throat. "That's what you think."

"Don't fucking push me." Grady suddenly snarled and was right up in Dresdon's face. "I might have had a rough time and a long journey, but I can still take your sorry ass on."

"Rough time. I heard the humans caught you. We've gone millennia without getting caught and then you … it's *you* who gets caught." He laughed but it was a nasty sound. "How pathetic."

"Could've happened to anyone, including you, ranger came out of nowhere and darted me."

"I ain't ever been in no zoo for the world to gawp at. You've put us all at risk. How can you be our alpha now?"

"They have no proof there are more of us or that we shift. I could just be a mutant from a gray. And besides, they'll be looking in Montana, not Canada or Alaska."

"I can't respect you, no one can, not after this." Dresdon jabbed his finger at Grady. "You need to go live as a loner, for everyone's safety."

"That's not gonna happen, and get your damn finger out of my face."

"What, this one?" Dresdon waggled his finger and made a strange snapping sound with his mouth.

This seemed to flick a switch in Grady and he lunged at Dresdon, fists flying and with all of his weight behind it. In an instant they were on the floor in a tangle of legs and arms. Fists connected with flesh and bone and grunts and huffs punctuated the air.

Tarl looked ready to join in, hopping from one

foot to the other, but he was hanging back, obviously waiting for a sign from his alpha.

"Oh, fuck," Billie said, rubbing her hands together. "Dresdon has really done it this time."

"What do you mean?" Sienna's heart was pounding. She didn't want Grady to get hurt and Dresdon was giving as good as he got.

The crowd were shouting and clapping. A few had shifted into direwolves and were now howling at the moon—a long, loud eerie sound that went on and on.

Grady took a particularly mean punch to the chin, his jaw clicking, but this seemed to send him into no-more-nice-guy and in an instant he had Dresdon on his back and pinned securely. He glared down at him, breathing fast, a drip of blood hung from his bottom lip. "You dare to question my authority?" he snarled breathlessly. "A youngster like you, no experience, a pain in my fucking ass?"

"Fuck you." Dresdon had spittle in the corners of his mouth.

"No, fuck you, try anything like this again and you'll be banished, Dresdon. The only reason I'm not doing that now is you'll starve on your own over the winter and we can't afford to lose numbers these days."

"Get the hell off me."

"You gonna stay in your lane?" Grady asked, not moving his weight.

"I said get off!"

Grady said nothing, just raised one eyebrow. The drip of blood fell and landed on Dresdon's cheek.

"Fuck, yeah, okay, you're back, you're alpha. I get it." The words seemed to scratch like glass over his tongue.

"Say it again."

"You're alpha, I get it. Now leave me the fuck

alone."

"Happy to, and stay out of my sight for the rest of the night." Grady suddenly sprang up and stood tall. He wiped the back of his hand over his lip, smearing blood.

Dresdon rolled over, got to his knees, and then pushed to standing with a groan. He brushed his palms over his black sweater, and then with head down, shoulders stooped, he wandered back the way he'd come.

The chatter soon rose as everyone took their seats and began eating stew again.

"Are you okay?" Sienna rushed up to Grady. Billie was close at her side.

"Yeah, honey, I'm fine. Sorry you had to see that."

"Don't worry about me." She touched his lip. "You took a few nasty punches."

"I heal quick. It's nothing." He set a kiss on her forehead. "Get some food, we've had a long journey."

Tarl was holding a wooden bowl steaming with delicious-smelling stew. "Here."

"Thanks." She took it.

"I hope you like it, I made it." Billie grinned at her.

"It's looks great and just what we need."

"Come, let's sit," Grady said, also taking a bowl of food.

"Tell me," Billie said, sitting close to Sienna. "Where are you from? How did you meet Grady and Tarl?"

"I'm from New York. And I met Grady in the zoo."

"The zoo?" Her eyes widened.

"I was his keeper." She looked at Grady who raised his eyebrows at her then spooned in food. "Not that he'd eat."

Billie shrugged. "It's the first rule. Get captured, starve to death to keep our secrets."

"Luckily I met Tarl before that happened and he explained to me what Grady was … what you all are, I'm guessing."

"I am, most of us are." Billie glanced around. "There are a few humans here in our circle."

Sienna nodded. "The guys have been trying to explain it all, since we broke Grady out, that is."

"You must be in some serious trouble for that."

"She sure is," Tarl said, "which is why she's here, forever, with us, as our woman, our mate."

"There's no going back," Grady said. "Sienna has made a huge sacrifice not just for me and for our pack but for the survival of direwolf."

"Happy to do it." Sienna nodded as the word "mate" rattled around her mind and reminded her that these men were also animals. "Really, I was … am."

"You're a very special person, I can tell." Billie beamed at her. "And I'm glad you're here, more females is always a bonus, we're outnumbered." She giggled. "But I knew you were coming, all of you, I could sense it." She nodded at a cabin to the right. "Which is why I got your place ready. There's food, clean sheets, and a fire waiting to be lit."

"You're a gem." Tarl grinned at her. "You really are."

Sienna studied Billie a little closer. She was young, definitely only just a teenager.

"I'll go light the fire now." Billie jumped up. "So, it's cozy."

"Thanks." Grady stood and helped himself to more stew from the pot over the fire."

"She's young," Sienna said to Tarl.

"Yes, she only started shifting this summer."

Sienna found herself watching Billie walk away and wondering what color direwolf she'd be.

"When we start shifting," Grady said, sitting down. "It changes all of our senses. We can smell more acutely, hear things we couldn't before, and at night we can see almost as well as during the day."

"And also," Tarl said, setting his finished food aside. "We get a wolf sense, one that guides us when we need it to. I think that's why I sat at your booth in The Gin Room that night, Sienna."

"And how Billie knew her alpha was returning." Grady took Sienna's hand and kissed her knuckles. "Are you ready to see your new home?"

"Yes." She looked into his eyes. "I am."

They left the group, several watching them go as though still checking it was real that their alpha was with them again and unharmed.

Several wooden steps led up to a porch with a seating area. It had been recently swept and a potted plant sat on the table.

Stepping through a large wooden door, Sienna was instantly surrounded in heat and the scent of pine needles. The large area was set with neat wooden furniture that included a big table, eight chairs, several soft seats before a fire, and a long thin kitchen along the back wall. The chimney breast was stone and opposite were stairs that led up to a mezzanine.

"What do you think?" Tarl asked, straightening one of the chairs at the table.

"It's a lot of wood." She laughed looking at the big horizontal logs that made up the walls and then the polished wooden floor.

"It's easy to source around here." Grady laughed and went to the refrigerator. He pulled it open. "Thanks for this, Billie, appreciate it."

"The eggs are fresh this morning, so is the bread, my mother made it for you."

"She's a gem." Tarl added a log to the fire Billie was tending. It was instantly licked my flames.

"I'll leave you to it." Billie stood and walked up to Sienna.

To Sienna's surprise she embraced her.

"I really am glad you're here. Tomorrow, I'll introduce you to the other women."

"How is Madeline?" Grady asked. "I didn't see her at the fire."

"She's due any day now." Billie nodded seriously. "And is staying in her cabin, resting."

"Ah, good, okay. Let me know as soon as she has the baby." Grady's expression fell. "It's a dangerous time for a woman but we'll do everything we can to keep mother and child safe. The Jeep has a full tank, right? In case we need to drive her to town, to the hospital."

"Yes, full to the brim. She'll be glad you're back holding the pack together, Grady. You too, Tarl, we missed you both." And with that Billie slipped from the cabin shutting the door behind her.

Tarl dropped his rucksack on the floor.

Sienna did the same, she'd almost forgotten she'd been wearing it.

"You want a shower?" Tarl asked her.

"Er, yes, that would be great." It had been a long day with a lot of hanging on to a huge wolf as they'd sped through forest and over plains.

"The shower room is up those stairs, next to the bedroom."

"Thanks."

Grady sat and began to undo his boots.

Tarl poked at the fire.

She grabbed her rucksack then wandered up the

stairs taking in the pictures that hung on hooks on the wall. Mostly they were of landscapes, though there was one of a direwolf howling at a full moon.

The bathroom was warm and clean and Sienna quickly showered and dried herself on a big towel that smelled freshly laundered, by Billie she presumed. She then pulled on some soft cotton pajamas, brushed her hair and teeth, and re-emerged.

When she looked down at the living area she paused and her breath hitched. Grady and Tarl were naked. They were lying on the fur rug in front of the fire, kissing. The glow of the flames caressed their strong bodies, highlighting their muscles and taut tendons.

She swallowed and a knot of excitement caught in her belly. But this time she didn't want to be a voyeur, so she went down the stairs, her bare feet silent.

They were kissing as they explored each other's bodies. Small moans catching in their throats. Grady took hold of Tarl's cock and pumped it slowly, root to tip.

"Fuck, yeah," Tarl murmured.

He opened his eyes and spotted her.

Grady also turned. "Join us," he said.

Sienna didn't need to be asked twice. She peeled off her pajamas then kneeled on the rug.

"Tarl has a great cock," Grady said, still working it. "You touch it too."

She did as instructed, her hand bumping up against Grady's. Tarl was steely hard and his shaft hot.

"He likes his balls tickled." Grady took her free hand and set it over Tarl's warm soft balls.

"Oh, fuck," Tarl said, flopping onto his back, almost sacrificial. "You know that's my undoing."

"Perhaps we want you undone." Grady chuckled.

Tarl groaned as Sienna worked his balls gently and added pressure to his cock, following Grady's lead.

His abdomen was tense and defined and he was breathing fast and shallow.

Grady caught her chin and urged her to look up at him. "You're perfect for us," he murmured and then kissed her. His tongue found hers and a shot of lust burst into her system. She wanted to feel Tarl come, she wanted Grady to fuck her. She wanted to watch the guys fuck too. She wanted it all.

"God, you're sexy," Grady said. "I so want to fuck you. I want you to be ready for me."

"What do you mean?"

He didn't answer, instead he looked down at Tarl. "You can come when you need to. You've got my permission."

"Thank fuck." Tarl gripped the rug and arched his neck. "I can't … fuck…"

Grady sped up, his movements fast and determined. "Don't stop, Sienna, don't stop with his balls."

Tarl was gasping for breath. His body a mass of tension. And then he came. Semen bursting onto his belly and a cry of ecstasy rattling around the room. His balls retracted and he canted his hips as though pounding into their hands as they worked his cock.

And then he flopped back, a full body tremor going from his legs to his jaw. "Oh, fuck, that was … the both of you, touching me."

"Yeah, we can tell you liked that." Grady chuckled and slowed. He leaned forward and kissed Tarl's chest, beside his right nipple.

Sienna recalled having both of their hands on her. It was very erotic to have the attention of two sexy people.

Tarl opened his eyes. "You're hard, Grady. Do you want—"

"To fuck, yeah, course I do." He turned to Sienna. "And I wanna fuck you."

"You have to tell her first." Tarl pushed to his elbows and a crease formed between his eyes. "You can't fuck her without telling her."

Chapter Nine

"Without telling me what?" Sienna asked and linked her fingers together. What other secrets did her men have? What other secrets could they possibly have?

Tarl was breathing fast, and said nothing as he looked expectantly at Grady. The shadows from the fire licked over his long body and the moment seemed to extend.

Grady shoved his hand through his hair. He was warm, a sheen of perspiration sat on his brow and in his underarm.

"What is it?" Sienna asked again.

"Because I'm alpha I have this thing..." Grady said.

"Thing?" She swallowed down a bolt of nerves. What could be so hard to tell her?

"My cock." He took his erection in his hand. "It ... it knots, when I enter a mate it flares, a lot, and that's it."

"What do you mean, that's it?" She studied his erect cock. It was very domed, the glans extra thick and wide. She'd thought he was just very well hung when she'd seen him in the shower before, but now she realized he was different.

"It's called knotting," Tarl said. "It's part of species survival. To ensure maximum chance of impregnation. Once he starts fucking, that's it, he's stuck inside until he comes."

She tipped her head and drew her attention back to Grady's face. She saw a flash of vulnerability in his eyes and cupped his cheek. "Isn't that the point? To fuck until you come? Until both partners come?"

"Yeah, it is, it just can feel a bit weird, that's all." Grady bit his bottom lip. "For the partner."

"Takes a while to get used to," Tarl said. "There's no pounding in and out, he's trapped in, trapped in deep."

"But you're used to it," Grady nodded at Tarl.

"Yeah, I love it." Tarl suddenly grinned. "Means there's always going to be a very satisfied Grady at the end of our fucking session."

Sienna leaned forward and kissed Grady, gently, on his lips. "If Tarl loves it then I will too."

"Are you sure?"

"I'm sure."

"I don't think it will take me long to come when we start fucking," Grady said. "I've been hot for you since you squirted into my palm earlier."

She felt her cheeks flush at the memory. "I have no control over that."

"And I have no control over my knotting cock." He raised his eyebrows.

"Are you ready to fuck him?" Tarl asked, sitting and cupping her right breast. He flicked her hard nipple with his thumb.

"Yes." Of course she was. Grady was big and sexy and she felt so close to him. "Do you usually ask Tarl if he's ready?"

Grady huffed. "No, if I want to fuck Tarl, I just bend him over fuck him, he's my beta."

"And me? Am I your beta?"

"No." He ran his hand into her hair and held her steady as he looked at her intently. "You're my woman. The only woman I'll ever want."

Her heart swelled. He felt the same as she did.

"The only woman *we'll* ever want," Tarl added.

"Oh…" she said on a sigh and shook her head. "I never could have predicted this new life but I'm so happy. I'm so excited for our future." Every word she spoke was true. The old Sienna who carefully considered her next move had well and truly gone, and she'd landed in Canada with a pack of shifters and finally felt at home.

"We're going to make you so happy, forever," Tarl murmured and kissed her. He encouraged her to lie on the soft rug. The fire warmed her flesh, as did Grady's kisses over her belly and up to her breasts. She relaxed into the moment of feeling safe and adored.

"You're so beautiful," Tarl murmured onto her lips. "The most beautiful woman in the world."

She stared up into his eyes. He was young and handsome but he wanted her and that was the truth, she could see it.

"And your body is perfect," Grady said, stroking over her belly and then between her legs.

"Oh, yes ... please, let's do this." She eyed his huge cock and wide slit. "I can do it."

"I know you can," Tarl said, tweaking her nipples just the way she liked.

Grady stroked through her folds, spreading her arousal. He found her entrance and dipped in. "You're gonna hug me so tight." He swallowed. "I can't fucking wait."

"So don't." She bucked her hips.

He filled her with two thick fingers and caught her clit with the heel of his hand.

"Oh, fuck." Her belly tensed. "I'm so turned on."

"I can tell." He went deeper and stroked over her G-spot. The hardness of his hand caught on her clit and he rubbed it with a firm rocking motion.

Her eyes fluttered shut and she moaned, her body a mass of sensation. Already she could feel herself getting wet and the pressure in her pelvis was beginning to mount.

"It's time," Grady said after a minute of stimulating her. "Fuck, yeah, it's time. Get on your hands and knees."

"My hands and…"

"It's best for him," Tarl said. "And we'll make it best for you too."

Grady helped her turn over. Her hair hung down and her knees and palms pressed into the soft fur rug.

"You have a damn cute ass," Tarl said, stroking over first her left and then her right buttock.

"So sweet." Grady ran his fingertip down her cleft, over her asshole and to her entrance. "I'm going in slow this first time, okay?"

"Yes." Her heart was thudding and her skin tingled as though she was more alive than ever before. Would she really be able to take him?

And then the head of his huge cock was prodding her entrance.

"Just relax," Tarl said, stroking her hair. "And it will feel amazing, I promise."

She blew out a breath as Grady pushed in. The flare of his cock tip stretched her internal flesh, pushing and filling her in a new dense way.

"Ah, yes…" she moaned, arching her back and encouraging him.

"Fuck, it's been so long since I was with a woman," Grady murmured, gripping her hips. "And now, you, this is perfect, you are perfect."

She pressed her lips together as the filling went on. His girth was solid and the length of him seemed to go on forever.

Eventually his warm, hairy balls pressed up against her pussy lips.

"I'm in," he said. "And staying in."

She shifted her hips and found that he was truly

lodged inside of her. Even if she'd wanted, she couldn't have made him slip out. He'd knotted deep in her pussy and would be there until he came.

"You've done it," Tarl said, slipping his fingers from her lower back, around to her waist and then lower, to circle her clit.

"Oh, yes, that … Tarl…"

"Come when you need to," Grady said. "Come as many times as you want."

She didn't think it would take much. To be so full of glorious hard cock and have Tarl working her clit was intense. She'd come soon, she was sure of it.

Grady began to move, not in and out but a rocking motion that shifted him inside her so that his cock rubbed over her G-spot.

She groaned and dropped to her elbows, let her forehead touch the rug. She'd surrendered to her men. She was theirs. They could do what they wanted with her and she knew it would be good. Damn good.

"Fuck, the scent of your arousal is intoxicating," Tarl said. "I could get drunk on it."

She didn't answer. The pressure was building, soon she'd need to release it. The heat and density in her pelvis would erupt and it would shake every bone in her body when it did.

A direwolf howled outside and a log slipped on the fire. The men continued to fuck her and finger her clit.

"I'm going to come," she gasped. "I am … nearly … nearly there."

"Yes, come." Grady tightened his hold on her hips. "Come and squirt, I want to feel that, fuck, yes, now … squirt at me with your tight fucking pussy."

His commanding voice and dirty words sent her over the edge and she let her orgasm release. Her pussy pulsed wildly around Grady's stiff cock and she felt the heated gush of liquid release. She cried out, a long wail of bliss, and her body shook.

Tarl kept circling her clit, extending the pleasure. "So fucking hot when you come," he said, excitement lacing his voice.

"You've drenched my cock," Grady said, his voice hoarse. "Oh, fuck, that's incredible … I'm … I'm coming."

He was pulsing inside her, filling her with his seed.

She gasped his name and pushed back onto his cock, wanting everything he could give her.

"Oh, yeah, oh, yeah…" Grady moaned and slapped up against her hard as he pulled her back onto him. "That's fucking it." He let out a strange, strangled cry that almost sounded like a howl.

"Jesus," Tarl said, slowing his efforts on her clit. "You're incredible together."

Sienna was warm, perspiration laced her skin, and her left side was hot from the fire.

"You did it." Grady ran his hands from her hips to her ass and set each palm over her cheeks. "You were brilliant."

"That was…" She was gasping for breath. Bright lights still flashed in her vision. "Incredible."

"It didn't frighten you?" Tarl asked. "That he was stuck inside of you?"

"No, it was the only thing I wanted at that moment, for him to be there, until he came. And my G-spot, fuck, that felt good."

"That's why I wanted you on all fours," Grady said. "For this first time at least. So you could feel it all."

"And there will be so many more times," Tarl said, kissing over her ear. "The winters are long, we have to entertain ourselves somehow."

"I like ... the sound ... of that." And oh, she really did.

"Give me a minute to deflate," Grady said. "I can't pull straight out, but it won't be long."

He must have been losing his erection to some extent because trickles of cum, or perhaps her own release, were making their way down her thighs. What was this new squirting thing? It certainly added to the intensity of her orgasms, she'd never come so hard and long as with Tarl and Grady. Luckily, they seemed to love it so that countered any embarrassment.

"Okay, just relax," Grady said, beginning to pull out. "I think it should be okay now but if it hurts, I'll stop."

Very slowly he withdrew, it didn't hurt but Sienna could feel every inch of him as he left her body. He'd been so deep, his cock so thick, that when he did pull away from her, she missed the sensation of fullness.

She flopped onto her stomach, too exhausted and sated to move. Suddenly there was a towel being wiped over her thighs, poking in between them.

"I'll sort this," Tarl said. "Then you can just sleep."

"Here?"

"For a while?" Grady pulled her into an embrace, her face settling into the crook of his neck.

She breathed deep, enjoying his scent and the roughness of his stubbled flesh.

"And then, when you've got your strength back, perhaps we'll move to the bed, go again, reckon it's my turn to fuck you," Tarl said, settling on her other side and tangling his legs with hers.

Sienna yawned and reached behind herself to touch Tarl. "I could be persuaded to go along with that plan."

       "Good." He kissed her nape. "But sleep now, you just took something not many people could."

Chapter Ten

One Month Later

Sienna woke to the sound of silence and a milky light streaming in from a crack in the curtains.

It had been snowing all night. A quiet blanket now lay over Kochi. It had been expected and she was excited to see the camp as a winter wonderland.

Tarl moved at her side, cleared his throat, and reached for her. "Morning, gorgeous."

"Hey." She glanced at the dent in the pillow to her right. "Where's Grady?"

"When it's the first snowfall, he likes to do an early patrol."

"Ah, I see." She knew this meant he'd shifted and gone out into the forest to survey the pack's territory.

"The snow gives up lots of secrets when it's fresh," Tarl went on. "Prints especially."

"Why didn't you go with him?" Usually, they went out as a pair, or sometimes as a pack, every shifter would go leaving the eight humans in camp alone.

"I wanted to stay with you."

"That's nice." She snuggled a little closer to his hard, muscle-bound torso.

"We were talking last night, when you fell asleep."

"About me?"

He chuckled. "Of course."

"And?" She looked up at him.

"From what we can gather, the search for you and Grady has died down, but it will never really go away and if they extend the search field they might come to

Canada."

She pushed up to her elbows and frowned. "Do you really think that will happen?"

"Honestly, no. I think the direwolf is old news, the authorities have better things to spend time and money on. But we need to keep you close. No going into town even though you'd like to."

She touched his chin, stroking over the little dink there. "I'm not really bothered about the town. I love it here at Kochi, it feels like home already."

He smiled. "That makes me happy to hear you say that."

"I am happy."

He kissed her. "I love you so much," he said onto her lips.

"And I love you." She pressed against him, her breasts flattening. She loved both Tarl and Grady with every beat of her heart. She'd never known such love in her life. It was as if she'd waited years for this to happen. And every moment of waiting had been worth it.

He deepened the kiss and pulled her closer still. His body was deliciously warm and the room felt magical, otherworldly, as if they were in their own little paradise.

"How do you wake up looking so good?" he murmured, stroking her hair from her face.

"And how do you always wake up with a hard-on?" She grinned and ran her hand from his chest, over his flat belly to find his erection.

"I have no idea." He laughed softly. "But if you want to put it to good use…"

"I think I do."

She kissed his cheek, then down his neck to the hollow of his throat, shimmying her body lower as she went.

He moaned softly and shifted the duvet, anticipating her next move.

She smiled to herself as her lips traveled over the hair from his sternum to his groin. His youthful vitality was as sexy as Grady's dominant confidence.

With the duvet cocooning her in darkness she found his cock and took it in her hand.

"Ah, yeah…"

Swiping her tongue over his slit, she felt his thighs tense and he let out a long sigh.

Feeling lazy and indulgent she kissed his shaft, exploring with her mouth and her fingers. There was no rush. His cock twitched and he slipped his hand downward to tangle his fingers in her hair.

She adored that feeling of being in control and him needing her so much. But still she didn't rush, taking her time before she took his cock tip into her mouth.

"Oh, God, yes." He groaned long and low.

She took him deep, adoring his flavor, his heat, and the solidity of his erection. He tickled the back of her throat and she stopped, held him there for a few seconds then pulled back up.

He tensed further and his cock twitched in her mouth.

Taking him again, hugging him with her tongue, she sought out his balls and cupped them gently. As she did so a drip of pre-cum leaked from his slit basting her mouth in salt.

He was nearer than she'd anticipated.

Suddenly she felt the need to make him come hard and fast. So she sped up, working him with her mouth and hands with determination.

He bucked his hips, cried out her name, and then in an instant was dragging her up the bed and throwing back the duvet.

"Not like that," he gasped.

"But…?"

"I want you to come too." He positioned her over him, moving her like she weighed nothing. "Ride me."

She folded her legs either side of his body and hovered her pussy over his cock. He was holding it up, ready for her to lower herself onto. "I would have been happy if—"

"I love watching you come," he said his eyes sparkling. "It's my favorite thing."

She smiled and set her hands on his broad chest, lowered herself onto him. The stretch was gloriously thick, only just the pleasure side of discomfort. And when her ass hit his thighs, she felt so full she barely knew where he ended and she began.

"Ah, yeah, that's it…" He gripped her legs and stared up at her. "Fuck, I love it when you do that."

"You do?"

"Hell, yeah. You're so gorgeous."

She rocked forward, connecting her clit with his hard body. "Oh…" She fluttered her eyes closed. This had been a great idea.

He urged her on and she set up a grinding rhythm, taking what she wanted.

"Fuck, you have me so near the edge," he said breathlessly. "You always do."

"I'm close," she said, not fighting the pressure that was growing rapidly. "I'm real close." She flung back her head, jutted out her breasts, and arched her spine.

His cock was so solid inside her, her clit swollen and needy.

"Sienna," he gasped. "Please…"

She came, crying out and butting her clit against him with more force. The bliss poured through her, going to her toes and fingers, and making her scalp tingle. So damn good.

He let out a long low groan that could almost have been a howl and bucked his hips as he dragged her onto him. He spurted inside her, his semen mixing with the pleasure gushing from her in a torrent of release.

He snapped upright, gathering her close and still coming. She was still coming, her orgasm extending, and as his mouth hit down on hers, bright lights flashed before her eyes.

Her heart was thudding, her pulse loud in her ears, and she gasped for breath.

"I've got you," he said, breaking the kiss and cupping her face. "I've got you."

She stared into his eyes. "I know."

They slowed and a tremor of satisfaction wended up her spine.

"That was a good way to start the day. Grady will be sorry he missed it."

"I enjoy our alone time." She touched his cheek, over a small freckle.

"You don't enjoy alone time with Grady?" He raised his eyebrows.

"Of course I do, it's just different. Just like it's different when the three of us are together."

"I understand."

"And I guess it's different when it's just you and Grady, right?"

He was quiet for a moment, then, "Yes, and it was just us for so long, before we met you, I guess there's a familiarity, a knowledge that we can get wild without scaring or hurting the other person."

"Wild?"

He laughed. "We are direwolves, could we be wilder?"

Sienna showered and then cooked eggs for breakfast, all the time peeking out the window at the snowy landscape. It really was beautiful. But as she sipped her coffee her mind wandered to what Tarl had said about it being wild when he and Grady were alone together, having sex.

She'd only witnessed it once, when Grady had just gotten out of the zoo, and he was still regaining strength, but he'd been dominant even then. Taking Tarl's hand and wrapping it around his erection, ordering him to "do it."

A little shiver of desire went through her, it was laced with curiosity and she hoped she'd get to witness them fucking wildly one day. Not worrying about her being with them, just basic, doing what their instincts drove them to do.

Knock. Knock.

"Got a visitor," Tarl said, standing.

"Yes, Grady wouldn't knock."

Tarl opened the door. "Hey, Billie."

"Hey, I've got bread for you, from Mom, and also Madeline is up for visitors today, she was exhausted yesterday, the baby had kept her awake all night."

"Oh, great news, and thanks for the bread." Sienna reached for a small cot blanket she'd been embroidering with thread Billie's mom had kindly given her. She created a design of zoo animals, though no cats of any sort, that wouldn't go down well. "I'll take this to her, it will come in handy now the weather has really turned."

"It will. I'll come with you." Billie smiled.

Quickly Sienna pushed her feet into her boots and pulled on her coat. "See you later." She kissed Tarl on the cheek.

As they crunched through the snow, Sienna

noticed the Jeep had gone, the tracks showing it had made for the lane through the forest.

"Hank went to town," Billie said, seeing the direction of Sienna's gaze. "To get supplies."

"Did he take my list?"

Billie laughed. "Of course, I gave it to him personally."

"Ah, good, I came with so little, I had what I thought I needed but there's always more, isn't there?"

"There is, though, only a few things are truly essential." She shrugged.

Dresdon appeared, stomping through the snow with an axe in his hand. He turned his attention away from them, neither glaring nor acknowledging. Sienna knew he was still pissed at being put in his place by Grady, and because she was Grady's woman, he didn't much like her.

"Don't mind him," Billie said. "He'll get over his sulk eventually, and if he doesn't Grady will send him to Alaska in the spring."

"Alaska?"

"There's another direwolf pack there, a bit bigger than this one. He'll have to fit in or they'll soon drive him out, they won't have as much loyalty to him as Grady has."

"You think Grady is loyal to him?"

"He didn't kill him, did he?"

"Are you serious?"

"Yes, alpha males do not like having their positions threatened, they'll fight to the death to protect it. Grady spared Dresdon the night you arrived, and a few of us were surprised."

"Were you?"

"No, I understand how important every direwolf is, there's not many of us, even bad-tempered ones like

Dresdon are important. He needs to find a mate and reproduce, that would be the most helpful thing he could do for his species."

They reached Madeline's cabin and Billie reached out to knock on the door.

"No," Sienna said catching her wrist. "I'm guessing the baby is asleep, don't wake him."

"Good idea." Billie lowered her hand and quietly opened the door. "Madeline?"

"Hey, yes, come in," a soft voice called.

They stepped into the embrace of the warm cabin and quickly removed boots and coats.

"Hey, Sienna, Billie, it's so nice to see you." Madeline was sitting by the fire holding a sleeping baby. The room smelled sweet and powdery and a vase of winter jasmine stood on the windowsill.

"Is he sleeping?" Billie asked.

"Finally." Madeline gently stroked the baby's thick dark hair.

"Shall I make you a drink?" Sienna asked.

"Yes, please, and for yourselves. Hank has gone to town with the lists."

"I'll make the drinks." Billie scooted to the kitchen area. "You give Madeline the present you made her."

"Present?" Madeline smiled at Sienna.

She was very pretty, blonde with a soft face and blue eyes. She was also human, not a shifter, and there weren't many in Kochi, so Sienna had felt an instant connection when she'd met Madeline a few weeks previously.

"I hope you like it, and I hope it comes in useful." She held up the blanket, letting it unfold to reveal the elephants, rhinos, monkeys, and giraffe she'd carefully stitched on.

"Oh, I love it, thank you." Madeline beamed.

"You're welcome, though I haven't had time to do anything like this for years. I've been so busy with work and…"

"Did you enjoy doing it?" Madeline asked.

"Very much so, I added some material and thread onto my list. It will be nice to do over the winter."

"It snowed heavily in the night," Billie said, setting down three steaming mugs on a small table.

"Yes, I know, but it's so pretty." Madeline nodded at the window.

"How long have you been here?" Sienna asked, reaching for a drink.

"This will be my second winter." She paused. "I really like the winter, that feeling of hibernation. And this year, all we have to do is stay in and be warm and cozy together." Again, she touched a tuft of her baby's hair. He didn't stir. "I don't have to worry about anything. Hank is such a great provider."

"How did you and Hank meet?" Sienna asked. "If you don't mind me asking."

"No, I don't mind." She smiled and glanced at the fire as though memories were flooding her thoughts. "My family owns a farm, about fifty miles from here. I used to spend a lot of time riding out, checking the boundaries, and I kept coming across this handsome guy, just hanging around, sometimes with a tent, sometimes not. He said he was fishing or trapping or something like that. I found myself going out hoping to see him, then actively looking, and he was always there."

"But you didn't know he was a shifter then?"

"No, not at all. I thought he was intriguing, not like the guys in the local town. He was confident, self-sufficient, and he seemed to really see me, do you know what I mean?"

Sienna nodded, she knew exactly what Madeline meant because it was how she felt when Grady and Tarl looked at her.

"One day, it was early winter, I was out on my own, horse tethered as I fixed a rail, and a grizzly came out of nowhere. I hadn't expected to see one, not that time of year."

"Oh, my goodness!" Sienna's eyes widened. "What did you do?"

"Nothing, except nearly pee myself with fright." She chuckled. "But before I could even think about my next move this huge wolf appeared. Nothing like the wolves I'd seen before—so much bigger, the head was huge, it was bigger than the grizzly—and it stalked up to it snarling with its hackles raised. The grizzly seemed to shrink in fear, like literally hunched in on itself. The wolf snapped at it several times, then the bear turned and ran into the forest. I'd never seen a creature retreat so quickly, it was clearly terrified of the wolf, and for a grizzly to be scared, I mean, they're top of the food chain, right."

"Right." Sienna nodded.

"Or so I'd thought, but now I'd seen a creature so big and mighty, the grizzly seemed insignificant. I stood there, shaking, waiting to meet my Maker. I was sure I'd be a nice morning snack for this wolf. But instead, he walked up to me, his blue gaze set firmly on mine and nuzzled his nose into my gloved hand. My heart was pounding, fear had made my legs turn to jelly, and I just stood there with a strange sense of having seen the wolf before, even though I knew I hadn't. Then he turned and ran back into the shadow of the trees."

"And then what?" Sienna asked taking a sip of her drink.

"No sooner had I gotten to my horse, Hank

appeared, he wore only jeans and boots, his torso bare. I was glad to see him and started to tell him about the bear and the wolf. He didn't say anything, just stared at me with his blue eyes—blue eyes I knew I'd seen before, only minutes ago. It was then I understood he was the wolf." She smiled and shrugged. "He didn't deny it so I knew it was true. We started dating and once he trusted me totally, and I'd agreed to live with him in his cabin in the woods, he showed me the truth. He showed me what he was. A direwolf."

"That is quite the story." Sienna took a deep breath. "And you've been here ever since?"

"Yes, and finally, we have a son."

"Who will begin to shift when he reaches his teens." Sienna looked at the baby again. Madeline had draped the new blanket over her lap and the baby's body.

"Yes, that will be a proud day."

There was sudden movement outside. Billie stood and went to the window. "Grady is here."

"He is?" Sienna stood and set down her finished drink.

"Yes, he's outside with Tarl."

"Do you need anything else?" Sienna asked Madeline.

"No, it's been lovely seeing you. Hank will be back soon. I've asked for some chocolate from town, I really fancy it."

"I don't blame you."

Sienna bid her goodbyes, donned her boots and coat, and slipped outside letting the crisp air fill her lungs.

Chapter Eleven

"Hey." Tarl smiled at Sienna. He still wore just the low-slung sweats he'd eaten breakfast in, nothing else. He didn't seem to feel cold like she did.

"All good?" she asked, heading down the steps of Madeline's cabin.

Tarl glanced at Grady who was in his wolf form. Huge and dark and puffing out breath from his wide canine mouth.

"You finished checking the boundaries?" Sienna asked Grady.

Grady walked up to her, his big pads pressing into the snow. He stopped just before her, his nose at her belly, and breathed deep. He suddenly looked at Tarl, his blue eyes keen and sharp.

"He wants me to go check something out," Tarl said with a slight frown. "Will you be okay if we're gone for a while?"

"Of course, but is there a problem?"

"No, no, some grays have wandered near, nothing to worry about, they just need a strong direwolf scent to turn them away, and two lots of scent are better than one."

"Oh, okay." She smiled. "I'll be in the cabin. Enjoy the forest, it's beautiful today."

"We will." Tarl dropped his sweats and kicked them to one side. He then stretched upward, his torso elongating and his limbs flexing. He then became a blur as his skin shifted to fur and his face became that of a direwolf.

Sienna would never tire of watching her men become direwolves. Each time she watched she saw something new. A foot that became a paw, a tail stretch out, but never did she see the whole thing, there was too much to look at.

Tarl stood before her and shook, as though settling into his direwolf body.

She smiled and stepped up to him. She almost had to go on tiptoes to tickle him between the ears the way he liked.

He gazed at her, but only for a moment because then Grady turned and took off. Tarl was quick to follow. His fur pressed sleekly back by his speed and snow kicking up behind him.

When they'd gone from sight, Sienna stooped and picked up the abandoned sweatpants and headed back to her cabin, her home.

She cleaned out the fire and stacked it ready for lighting later. She sliced the bread and then prepared vegetables for a stew she planned to cook slowly in the oven. She then made the bed and tidied the bathroom.

Soon the short daylight hours were coming to an end and when she looked out, the lilac-hued shadows were stretching over the snow. Hank had returned, his Jeep parked in the usual spot, and most of the cabins had smoke curling from their chimneys.

Grady and Tarl had been gone a long time. The forest was still, not even a bird, and the sky above was dense with dark snow-filled clouds that seemed to be further pressing the light from the day.

It was time to get the fire going so the cabin would be warm and welcoming when her men came home.

Just before she turned from the window, she spotted movement in the trees. And then, from the darkness, burst her two big direwolves. They were running, but not full pelt, as though they were enjoying life, enjoying the cold day and being free.

She smiled, knowing how much they loved forest runs together. It was a balm to them, a way of burning off energy. She hoped they'd had a good day.

They charged toward the cabin, Tarl rounding the logs in the central clearing, Grady jumping them. Their fur was damp and they were breathing hard.

Pausing to straighten a cushion on the bed, Sienna heard the front door open and close with a slam. But the slam wasn't the last bang, it sounded as if furniture was being tossed around.

Quickly she went to the top of the stairs, dropped to a squat, and looked down at the living area.

They'd shifted already, back to their naked human form, and were kissing with frantic urgency. Her heart rate picked up and she gripped the railing of the staircase. They were hot for each other, wildly hot for each other.

Grady was in charge, that much was clear, even though Tarl was gripping his mate's ass with both hands. Grady shoved at another chair, knocking it out of the way, and stepped Tarl backward to the table. He caught Tarl's jaw in his hand, held him still. "I fucking love you."

"I love you too."

"This is the start, you know, of everything, for all of us."

Sienna was breathing fast, her belly a tense knot of excitement. They must know she was there … didn't they?

Either way they carried on. Grady captured Tarl's mouth in a kiss that had Tarl moaning as he gripped Grady's shoulders.

And then Grady suddenly spun Tarl around and shoved him so he was bent double over the table. The table legs scraped on the floor, a chair tipped over, they didn't seem to notice.

Tarl let out a gasp as Grady kicked his legs apart while keeping one hand between Tarl's shoulders, pinning him just where he wanted him.

Sienna's attention went to Grady's cock. He was fully erect, the thick end glossy and jutting forward.

"Get ready for it," he growled at Tarl. "Get fucking ready."

"Yes, yes, I'm ready." Tarl screwed up his eyes and gritted his teeth.

He'd braced himself, and Sienna wondered how many times they'd done this, over that table, before she'd arrived.

Grady licked the palm of his hand, wet his cock, and then pulled at Tarl's right ass cheek. "I'm going in," he said hoarsely, "and you're gonna come so hard."

"Yes. I want that." Tarl curled his hands over the edge of the table and arched his back. "Fuck me."

Grady didn't answer. He found Tarl's asshole and shoved in—a hard, almost brutal thrust to full depth.

They both cried out, the sound uninhibited, feral, desperate.

Sienna pressed her fingers between her legs. This was the most erotic thing she'd ever seen. They were rough and crazed for each other, it was different from how they were with her, as if they knew they couldn't hurt each other even in the most unleashed moments.

"You feel that?" Grady huffed as he rocked harder against Tarl. "You feel my big knotted cock, huh?"

"Oh, God, yes, I feel it … fuck." Tarl reached beneath himself for his cock and began to jerk off. "Fuck … yes."

Grady flung back his head, eyes closed and ground against Tarl, moving his cock inside of him, working toward his orgasm. His belly was taut, his chest hair dotted with perspiration and the tendons on his neck roped. He groaned and squeezed Tarl's buttocks, his fingertips pressing deep. Tarl groaned long and low and bucked back for more.

Sienna pressed on her clit through her pants. She was so turned on watching them, her clit swollen and her pussy quivering.

"You feel so damn good," Grady groaned. "I'm gonna fucking come so high inside you."

"Yes, yes, come…" Tarl let out long guttural groan.

Sienna recognized it as his getting to the point-of-no-return groan. He was giving into his release. There was no holding it off.

And then Grady brought his hand down on Tarl's right buttock in a hard stinging slap.

Tarl cried out and then was coming hard. He jerked his cock, cum landed on the floor and the side of the table. His face was contorted in ecstasy and his body granite hard.

"Ah … yes, squeeze me with your asshole like that…" Grady pulled his lips back in a grimace. "So damn good."

Sienna held her breath, excitement winging around her body and making her nipples tingle.

"Fuck, yeah!" Grady thrust harder into Tarl, shoving him up the table, skittering the table further across the floor. Another chair tipped over. "That's it." He tipped his head back again and howled as he pulsed in Tarl's ass.

Tarl was still clinging to the table, his body flushed now and his ass cheek bright red.

Grady kept coming, groaning with each spasm that wracked his body. The ecstasy radiating from him was palpable.

Sienna was sure a small orgasm rippled through her pussy, one that had emerged just from watching the two men she loved have wild, passionate sex.

Grady slowed and some of the tension went from his body.

Tarl had slumped onto the table, as though all his energy had been sucked from him.

"My beautiful beta," Grady said, tipping forward and kissing Tarl's neck. "You are such a good tight ass fuck, you know that?"

Tarl laughed suddenly, his body shaking. "I'm glad you think so."

"Always." Grady tenderly stroked Tarl's hair from his brow. "I'm gonna see if I can pull out now."

Tarl nodded and kept his eyes closed.

Very gently, delicately, Grady withdrew his cock. Once out, he wiped his forearm over his brow then reached for Tarl and drew him to standing. "Get dressed, we need to speak to Sienna."

She gulped and stood. "I'm here."

They both looked up at her.

A smile stretched on Tarl's face. "You watched?"

"You knew I was here. I told you I would be."

"Yeah, we knew where you were." Grady squeezed Tarl's shoulder. "And I'm glad you've seen that side of us."

She descended the stairs. "You're rough." She looked at Grady.

"He can take it, you, on the other hand, are more delicate." Grady reached for a pair of pants and pulled them on. "But maybe you'll let me fuck your ass one day, after…"

"After?"

Tarl looked at Grady, a flash of uncertainty crossed his eyes.

"What?" she asked. "After what?"

Tarl grabbed his sweats and stepped into them.

"We know something about you," Grady said. He took both of her hands in his.

"What?" She looked from Grady to Tarl and back to Grady. Fear suddenly caught in her throat? "Is it the authorities, did you find something on your run?"

"No, no," Tarl said quickly. "It was something Grady noticed before our run, when you were standing outside Madeline's cabin."

She frowned. "What are you talking about?"

"I could smell a new life," Grady said, "when I was in wolf form."

"Well, of course, Hank and Madeline's new baby was close by. And he's so adorable, honestly, such a sweet baby." She smiled.

"No," Grady said. "It wasn't their baby I could smell … it was ours."

"I … I don't understand."

Tarl stepped close and curled his arm around her waist. "Grady smelled the subtle change in your aroma, Sienna, you're pregnant with our child."

"Pregnant? But…?"

"Human contraception is no match for direwolf sperm." Grady tipped her chin so she was looking up at him. "And it doesn't matter if it is mine or Tarl's biological child, it's ours, our baby shifter is growing in your belly."

Automatically she set a hand over her lower abdomen. "But I don't feel any different, I…" Was her period late? Yes, a little, but she'd just put tampons on her shopping list so it was due soon or … or maybe not.

"Trust me," Grady said. "There is a baby in you, tiny, yes, but he or she is there."

Suddenly she felt a little dizzy and she leaned into

Tarl.

"It will be okay, we're together, in love, that's all we need," Tarl said holding her against his body.

She closed her eyes. "I know, and seeing Madeline with her baby I realized it's something I want in the future, but this … this is fast." She looked from Tarl to Grady.

"We've been fucking like it's going out of fashion," Grady said with a chuckle. "Every day, a few times a day, into the night."

"Before breakfast." Tarl raised his eyebrows at her.

She nodded. It was true.

"You're happy about it, right?" Grady asked. "The baby."

"Yes." The word came out fast and certain. "Nothing would make me happier than to be the mother of your child." She reached for them both. "And I may have given up my career at the zoo, but isn't this more meaningful, to be helping populate a near-extinct species? Right here, in my body I am helping and creating and…" Her eyes filled with tears. "This is the most amazing news, and I promise to look after my precious cargo."

"The baby will be here in six months," Tarl said. "It will be quicker than a normal pregnancy."

"Six months, that's the spring. We'll have a busy winter getting ready." She smiled, then laughed. "I am so happy."

"And so are we." Grady kissed her.

Tarl leaned close, his nose touching hers, then he was kissing her too. And then it turned into a heavenly three-way kiss that sent her heart overflowing with love and joy and excitement for the future.

She was a long way from New York City, Central

Park Zoo, and The Gin Room, but she was home and she'd found not just love but an important purpose in life with direwolves, creatures she'd believed to be extinct but were now her reason for waking up each day.

She was a very lucky woman!

The End

VOLUME ONE

SHIFTING HEARTS

Monsters of New York

Jade Marshall

Copyright © 2025

Chapter One

Akasha LaVey

Wherever Dreams May Lead

"I need to do this. Whether it makes sense to you or not," I say to my mother as I load the last of my belongings into the little red hatchback I have been driving for the better part of three years.

"I just don't understand why you need to move across the damn country," she says for the millionth time since I told her I was leaving, her hands firmly on her hips.

"It's only six hundred miles," I say with a sigh, rolling my eyes. "It's been six months since the dreams started. I need to find out where this will lead."

I don't mention the fact that I found my long-term boyfriend cheating on me last night. I wanted to leave before that incident, I just didn't know how to end things with him. I would have preferred to end on decent terms, but he made a different choice. Namely, a waitress from the local diner.

I still don't know how the fire in his room started. I was so angry that I somehow missed how or where the flames erupted from but at least no one was hurt.

"How do you know it will lead you anywhere? How do you know you're not just chasing something that doesn't exist?" my mother asks, drawing me back to the present.

My heart breaks just a little at the words she has been saying to me my entire life. I know she doesn't believe in the dreams I have, but I do, and as my mother I wish she would support me. After twenty-five years she knows the truth even if she won't admit it to herself or out loud.

My dreams are always more than they seem. From predicting my father's car accident and death three weeks before it happened when I was twelve, to knowing about my cousin's pregnancy and marriage six months before she met her husband. It's not always a life-altering prediction but when it is, you can take it to the bank.

"I know you don't want me to leave," I say softly. "But this is my life. I know in my heart this is the right thing to do."

"I just don't want you to get hurt," she replies. "What if it doesn't work out?"

"It will."

"But…"

I know she is simply being overprotective, but I need to shut her down.

"If I get to New York and there isn't anything there for me, I can always come back home." I stare at her intently, waiting for her to finally accept this is happening.

I know what waits for me in New York. A job and an apartment, and maybe even something life changing. I may say I'll return home but I have a feeling I will never return to Yellow Springs. My dreams are leading me to the city and something more, even though I'm not sure what that is yet. It's all still very disjointed but I trust the process.

"Yes, you can," she says, pulling me tightly against her chest and hugging me for long moments. "You can always come home, Akasha."

****

The drive is long. It takes almost three days to make my way from Yellow Springs to New York City. It probably would have been a shorter drive if I hadn't stopped to see all the sights along the way. But I've never been on a road trip and I don't know when I will get the opportunity again, so I make the best of it, even if I am doing it alone.

I stop at the Harman Rock Gardens in Springfield, I eat one of best burgers I've ever had on the hood of my car staring out at Buckeye Lake. I go shopping at Black Cat Vintage in Cambridge and eat a Chimichurri steak at West Texas Roadhouse in St Clairsville, before I finally make my way to the small apartment in Brooklyn I will live in from now on.

I was lucky to get a job at The Gin Room which includes the apartment. I did four interviews on Zoom a while back and I honestly didn't think I got the position. That is, until I was contacted last week.

Stepping out of my car I stare up at the four-story building, taking in the sights and sounds around me. It's my first time in a big city and I can't wipe the smile from my face. I can feel the energy thrum around me, and I wonder if it's like this for everyone.

"Akasha!" a woman with bright purple hair calls from across the road as she waits for the traffic to pass.

I wave, remembering her from one of my interviews.

"You made it," she says with a wide smile as she hugs me.

It's a strange sensation, being hugged by this unknown woman, but it also feels weirdly normal. That makes absolutely no sense but there it is. Her frantic energy feels like a healing balm to my battered soul.

"I'm so happy to see you. I got your message this morning and I've been waiting for you." She talks a mile a minute as she grabs my hand and leads me into the building. "Aldron, the owner at The Gin Room, owns five apartments in this building which he uses for staff. I have an apartment a floor below you."

She pulls me into the elevator, and I marvel at the strength such a pixie-like person possesses. As soon as we stop on the third floor, she is pulling me behind her once more until we reach a black door with a golden number in the middle: 3C.

She quickly opens the door and allows me entrance. My mind is blown the moment I walk inside. I was expecting a tiny apartment, but this place is massive. Beautiful wooden flooring, light grey walls, and lots of windows allowing in the natural morning light. The one-bedroom apartment is furnished sparsely and bigger than most people's houses, and I can't believe I will be living here.

"Um…" My words peter out. I don't know her name.

"Shit. Sorry, I got overexcited," she says with a bright red blush, extending her hand toward me. "My name's Arina. But everyone calls me Ari."

"Akasha," I say shaking her hand. "There must be a mistake, though."

"Mistake?" A frown mars her perfect features.

"I'm just going to bartend. This apartment must be for someone else."

She pulls her cell phone from her pocket before showing me the screen.

Name: Akasha LaVey
Position: Bartender
Apartment: 3C

"I don't think so," Arina says with a smile. "Is there something wrong with the apartment? Aldron doesn't mind if you change anything as long as you don't burn the building down."

Uncontrollable laughter bubbles out of me before I can stop it. Memories of the fire in my ex's apartment pop into my head.

"This place is bigger than the house I grew up in." She stares at me in confusion. "It's perfect," I say with a smile.

"Awesome! Let me help you unload your car and then I will show you around."

VOLUME ONE

Chapter Two

Korvin Slater

Enough is Enough

My skin feels too tight across my frame when I wake up. I had the same dream again. A woman in a translucent white dress beckons to me, a siren singing her song and luring me to her. Confusion swirls in my mind as my painful erection begs for attention.

For weeks I have woken up in a state of arousal. The thing that pisses me off is the fact that I don't even know what the woman in my dreams looks like. It's like there is a permanent shadow obscuring her face from my view.

I do know that she has a body made for sin. The dress she wears does nothing to hide her from my hungry gaze. Caramel skin, thick thighs, large breasts, and a softly rounded stomach are always visible. Other men might consider my dream siren to be fat, but all I see is a woman built to be fucked. As a black bear shifter, I must be careful when it comes to choosing sexual partners. Even in my human form I am a big motherfucker and could easily hurt someone.

Wrapping my left hand around my engorged erection, I stroke slowly, remembering every moment from my dream. The way she said my name, the sway of her breasts as she walked closer to me, the smell of sunshine and lavender that I couldn't escape even if I wanted to. I know I am dreaming of my fated mate. I also know that until I find her in my waking life, the woman in my dreams will remain faceless.

Closing my eyes, I allow my imagination to take

over.

The flimsy white material drops from her shoulders to pool at her feet, leaving her naked before me. Her nipples are large, a dusky brown color, tempting me to suck on them until they turn dark. Her pussy is covered by a smattering of perfectly trimmed hair but that doesn't stop me from seeing the moisture gathering there.

My hand moves faster, harsher over my length as I imagine her touching me, and moments later my cum explodes, landing on my stomach.

"Fuck," I grumble.

This shit needs to end, sooner rather than later. Not that I know how to do that. I will continue to dream of her until I have her in my life, and I don't even know where the fuck to start looking for her. Even if she is in New York, I may never meet her. Hell, she could be in Brooklyn, and I still might miss her. There are just too many people in the city for me to go searching for her. Perhaps if I had her scent, it would be different.

Someone knocks on the door to my apartment, and I can't help the anger that surges through me. Everyone knows to leave me the fuck alone. I'm a loner and I prefer it that way.

That's a lie. I constantly watch the people around me, wishing to have what they have. I want love, family, friendship. But at forty-five, I have all but given up on having any of those things. I am everything black bears are known for—ornery, short-tempered, aggressive. It's why I am so good at my job. I constantly have to fight to keep my beast under control, never allowing him a moment to take over.

Swinging my legs from the California king, I slide a pair of grey sweatpants up my legs, grab a towel, and clean the mess on my stomach before heading through my apartment.

"What?" the word falls from my lips as I open the door, and I instantly regret them. Arina stands on the other side with a massive smile.

She pushes the cup of fragrant coffee against my chest before making her way inside. She is the only person that doesn't fear me. In fact, she has gone out of her way to make friends with me even though I keep pushing her away.

"We have a new bartender."

"And?"

"I need you to be nice to her," she says hopping onto the marble kitchen counter.

I grunt, taking a sip of the bitter, black coffee she brought. How she knows my preference is beyond me, but I won't be complaining.

"I'm not a child, Ari. I know how to treat people."

She laughs, a light, happy sound. "Of course you do. That's why everyone in the building, at work, and even on the street avoids you."

"Whatever," I say with a growl. "You've said your piece, you can leave now." I gesture toward the still open door, but the little pixie doesn't move.

"She doesn't know about the paranormal world," she says softly.

"What?" I all but roar. "How could Aldron employ a human?"

"She isn't human, per se. She's just oblivious."

"Meaning?"

I wish she would just spit out what she has to say and get the hell out of my apartment. I need to be at The Gin Room in two hours and I still need to get in a workout and shower before then.

"She's a descendant of the witch, Marie Laveau, though I doubt she even knows it. I did a full ancestral search of her family and somewhere along the line they changed their last name to LaVey to distance themselves from the past," she explains. "She also doesn't know what she is capable of."

"Fuck my life." I run my hand over my beard with a shake of my head. "And you think it's a good idea to have a natural, untrained, oblivious witch in a bar full of shifters, vampires, ghouls, demons, and a million other things?"

"Aldron does." With those words she finally moves from her seat, basically skipping through the door. "See you later."

This is a very fucking bad idea. I can feel it in my bones. But The Gin Room belongs to Aldron, and he makes decisions that suit him. The rest of us can either fall in line or fuck off.

****

The fight is over before it even begins.

Even after an hour-long punishing workout, my bear is still agitated, roaming the corners of my mind. I have always struggled to control him. I think it's because I never had anyone to teach me how.

After my mother was killed in her animal form by a hunter, I was left alone in the world. I had to make my own way and learn how to control my animal, which I've always only had a tenuous grip on.

It's why I fight in the cage beneath The Gin Room. Every Friday for the past three years I face any willing opponent and let out all my suppressed rage to keep my bear happy. The violence and aggression I dole out in the cage make him happy. When I started, I fought in my animal form, but those fights are to the death. Killing someone, whether in their human or animal form, starts to take a toll on you eventually. Now, I only fight to submission or knockout and always in my human form.

The jaguar shifter across from me smirks, thinking he has my number after landing a single blow to my jaw. He fails to understand the fact that pain only drives me and my beast to more violence.

When he tries to hit me again, I quickly catch his fist before applying pressure. The scream that rends the air as I crush the bones in his hand has a deranged smile playing across my features. Within seconds he admits defeat, tapping out.

Another victory. Hollow as it may be.

I haven't even broken a sweat. If I get lucky, Aldron will find me another opponent for tonight. But for now, I need to allow others to fight.

I grab a quick shower in the back and dress in jeans and a dark blue t-shirt before making my way upstairs to the main bar. I rarely go into the bar but tonight I feel a strange pull toward the upper level. Pushing open the door I step into the full room, people milling about and socializing with each other. There is something different tonight, though, and I struggle to put my finger on what that is.

My gaze moves around the room, seeing some of the regulars, our bouncers, the twin Minotaur shifters, and Ari where she stands behind the bar handing out drinks.

The moment my eyes land on the new woman, I have to place my hand against the wall to keep my knees from giving out. Beautiful caramel skin, a mesmerizing smile, dark eyes, and unruly curls. The scent of sunshine and lavender wraps around me just like it does in my dreams. My bear roars in the recesses of my mind, fighting to go to her.

Her gaze collides with mine and I feel the magic flow between us. The room around us melts away and we are the only two people in the building, even though I know there are others around us.

It takes everything I have inside me to break the connection between us and stumble back downstairs. My control on my beast is slipping and I can feel the change coming over me with every step I take away from her.

I need to get away. I can't take the chance at hurting her, at letting my bear hurt her when my control finally snaps. She is my fated mate, and I will never allow anyone to harm her.

Especially not me.

Chapter Three

Akasha LaVey

First Day Jitters

For my first shift at The Gin Room, Ari and I go in an hour early. She wants to introduce me to the staff and show me around before it gets busy. Starting a new job on a Friday is a little strange to me but I'm not about to argue. Tonight will be fast and furious, a trial by fire.

Our uniform is made to accentuate the curves of a woman. A blood red strappy top with a black corset-like sleeveless overcoat, black skinny jeans, and charcoal flats complete the ensemble. I feel both sexy and comfortable which is another strange combination that works. I have only been in the city for a few hours and already I feel like a changed person.

Ari and I walk the three blocks from the apartment building to the bar. As we walk, I can't help but take in everything around me. Everything is larger than life and completely unfamiliar but beautiful in a way I would struggle to explain.

When we reach The Gin Room, I stare up at the ten-story red brick building after we walk down a long alley.

"The building has been in Aldron's family since 1818, when his great-great-great-great-grandfather came over from Europe," Ari tells me. "Originally, it was a factory or something, but it was empty for a long time. Aldron converted it into The Gin Room on the ground floor and apartments on most of the other floors, although there are also some offices spaces. The top floor is where he lives."

"That's kind of cool. The history and all that."

"It is," she says with a smile before leading me inside.

The interior is dimly lit, and it takes my eyes a moment to adjust but once they do, I can't hold back my gasp. It is massive and luxurious, not at all what you'd expect from the outside. There are seating areas with leather couches, aged wine barrels with high seating, and a massive bar running down the back with more seating. Even from here, I can see that the bar is a dark cherry wood with a stunning polished sheen.

Mirrors and frames with black-and-white photographs line the walls, all with gilded frames that look insanely expensive.

"Let me introduce you," Ari says, taking my elbow and leading me to a table full of men. "This is Knox and Cruz. The twins are here to keep people from causing problems."

"Hello," they say in unison, and I can't help but smile.

"This is Nyland." She gestures to the other man at the table. "He is our manager. He is Aldron's right-hand man and can help you with anything."

I smile at him as well but all he does is grunt. He doesn't even look at me, instead keeping his gaze focused on his phone.

Arina leads me across the room and behind the bar. She shows me where everything is and explains the single signature drink, The Bees Knees. Everything seems simple enough and just like any other bar I've worked in.

"You'll do fine," Arina says with a grin I can't help returning.

Soon enough the first customers trickle in. Three waitresses, in identical uniforms to ours, serve the lounging areas, but all the other patrons order from the bar. Energy thrums through the room and I feel I am soaking it in through my skin.

The customers are friendly and welcoming, introducing themselves and chatting while I get their drinks. Coming from a small town, I always assumed people in the city would be aloof and disconnected from one another, but everyone here seems to know each other. With all the different faces and conversations, the time passes quickly.

Three women stand at the bar, drinking shots, celebrating something. They laugh and chat, often including me in their conversation in one way or another. The center woman is slightly drunker than her friends and I know I will have to cut them off sooner rather than later. The moment the thought crosses my mind, I hear the crash of glass as she drops her cocktail on the surface of the bar.

I don't know how she did it but there is a lot of blood pouring out of her hand. Grabbing a clean towel, I wrap it around her hand and apply pressure.

"Get the first aid kit," I call to Arina only to see her already holding the little white box with the red cross in her hands.

The other patrons are watching us intently. My hands are holding the towel firmly around her wounded hand. For a split-second I wonder if I am applying too much pressure as the tips of my fingers tingle.

Slowly, I pull the towel away, hoping to clear enough blood to see where she cut herself. Shock courses through me as I clean her hand. There is no wound. How the hell is that possible? I turn her hand over again and again, looking for the injury that caused her to bleed all over the surface of the bar, but I can't find one.

My gaze collides with Arina's who just shrugs

before stowing the kit beneath the bar and continuing toward her waiting customers.

"Thanks, Doll," the woman says in a sultry voice, a small smile tugging at the corner of her mouth.

She hands me a hundred dollars before disappearing from the bar with her friends. My mind is still reeling with what just happened, trying to figure out how there was so much blood with no wound, when the atmosphere in the bar changes.

The air is electric, and my skin feels like it is being caressed. I scan the room to find out what the hell is happening. My gaze collides with a pair of dark eyes and for a moment I feel like I am alone with him in the bar, the entire world. My dream comes back to me, and I recognize those dark, tortured eyes.

I take in the man. He is tall, almost 6'5", with broad shoulders and a bulky build. His arms are thick and for a moment I wonder what it would feel like to have them around me. His t-shirt is fitted, showing off his pectorals and the slight rounding of his stomach. This man is fit but not like a boy would be. He is all muscle and bulk, not six-packs and cut muscles. He has a thick beard on his square chin and even with the low light I can see he is greying at his temples while the rest of his hair is pitch black.

I want to go to him, introduce myself. But just as quickly as he appeared, he is gone. My heart hurts and I feel bereft. I rub at the center of my chest. Even when I caught my boyfriend cheating, I was never heartbroken, but that's exactly what this feels like.

Chapter Four

Korvin Slater

Like a Coward

I run from The Gin Room. Like a coward I let my wobbly legs carry me as far away as I can get. And I do it quickly. I need to get away from the woman, the people, everything, before my bear pushes through to the forefront. I can feel my control slipping and I need to be alone when I let him out.

I rarely let my bear have free reign, but I know I need to let him out before he goes on a rampage in the city. I jump in my fire-engine-red pickup truck and drive. I head east toward New Haven where Forest Park is located. It may not be much but it's the closest place I will be able to shift and give my bear the freedom he so badly craves. I know other shifters who frequent this area, but they aren't really what I am worried about.

Thank God it's after midnight and I don't have to worry about a hundred humans being in the park at this time of night. If I'm lucky, I will be completely alone.

The drive is quiet as I fight to keep from letting my hairy foot get me pulled over. The last thing I need tonight is to be detained by the police, especially not with my bear dancing around beneath the surface.

It takes less than an hour, with traffic, to get to where I want—no, *need*—to be. I park hurriedly and jump out before tearing ass into the small forest. I walk for five minutes before I start stripping, knowing I will need my clothes to get home even though I always keep a spare set in my truck just in case.

My bear roars in the recesses of my mind,

unhappy with the pace. He wants out. Now.

The moment my sneakers are off and my jeans hit the dirt, the magic flows over me, my bones and muscles snapping, elongating, and realigning to suit the new, larger form of my bear.

I have been shifting for most of my life, and it doesn't hurt the way it used to, but I am still uncomfortable during and after the shift. But once I am in my animal form, I have never felt so free, I have never felt more like I am exactly where I am supposed to be.

My bear roars loudly, stretching out to his full seven feet. He scents the area around us before making a beeline back to my truck. In my mind I beg him to understand, to know that I am doing what is best not only for both of us, but for our curvy little mate. If we ever want her to be ours, we will need to work together instead of against each other. I can't—won't—put her in danger, even from us.

I can see the truck just through the tree line when he finally slows to a stop. He growls lowly before turning back to the foliage that offers us sanctuary. He turns to the nearest tree and slams his claws deep, leaving long trails as he moves down the length.

I would prefer not to leave any evidence of our visit. It won't be easy to explain the bear claw marks when the ranger finds it, but if this is how he chooses to let out his aggression I won't be saying a goddamned word about it. He can fuck up as many trees as his big black heart desires.

****

The moment I step into building I know she is here. How I missed it earlier is beyond me, but her scent is everywhere. In the lobby, the elevator, even the damn hallway. It's enough to have my bear tearing at my insides once more. It's a struggle to get from the elevator to my apartment, but once I'm inside I can finally breathe again.

"I know," I mumble, talking to my bear for the first time. "I want to go to her too, but we need to do this right. Not just barrel our way into her life."

In the recesses of my mind, my bear huffs and I can't help but chuckle.

I've never communicated with him. Seems tonight is filled with firsts for me. For both of us.

VOLUME ONE

Chapter Five

Akasha LaVey

The Bear

I know I'm dreaming but it feels more real than any single moment in my entire life ever has. A massive black bear stands in a meadow filled with wildflowers. He stares at me intently, not moving a single muscle except to breathe. For some reason I can sense fear rolling off him and I want to laugh at the complete absurdity of the thought. Why in heavens name would a black bear be afraid of me?

Turning in a circle I take in the forest that surrounds the meadow, looking for the threat that surely must be there. I can't think of anything else that would have a black bear feeling fear. But we are alone.

Turning back, I look to where the black bear stood but he isn't there anymore. Instead, he stands closer to the edge of the trees. He shakes his head and for a moment I think he is beckoning me to follow him as he moves between the tall trees. It only takes a split-second for me to decide before I am moving across the field, my hands skimming the tops of the tall grass and the flowers that grow in between.

"Hello?" I call out, hoping someone will answer me. "Is there anyone here?"

Birds sing their song in reply to my ridiculous question. A chuckle escapes me at the absurdity of everything going on around me.

"Why would you follow him?" a voice asks from behind me.

Turning, I all but trip over my own feet. I feel

myself falling and clench my eyes shut but I never hit the ground. Instead, strong arms band around my waist, and I find myself drawn against a broad chest. I stare at the expanse of naked skin before making my way up, along the column of a muscular neck, over a dark beard, until I reach a set of the darkest, most soulful eyes I have ever seen.

My breath lodges in my throat as I take in the man I saw earlier tonight at The Gin Room. His scent surrounds me, woodsy and fresh, and my entire body breaks out in a shiver. Dear God, he is even more handsome up close. I fight to keep my hands from running through his long, dark hair as he frowns down at me.

"Why would you follow him?" he asks again.

"Who?" I ask, my voice barely a whisper.

"The damn bear." He frowns, irritation lacing his words.

"What bear?"

His frown deepens into a full-on scowl. "There was a big ass black bear in the meadow. And the moment he disappeared into the trees you decided to join him."

"Oh, that. He invited me."

"Invited you?" he asks with a quirked brow.

I enjoy having his arms around me for a moment, breathing in his intoxicating scent. I wiggle in his grasp, feeling his erection against my belly. A rush of heat flows through me as arousal dumps into my system.

His eyes darken even more as he releases me, stepping back. It's only then I notice he is fully nude. His thick cock stands erect, pre-cum coating the crown, and I can't help but lick my lips. I wonder what he would taste like.

His large, scarred hands obscure my view as he tries to cover himself but fails miserably. My gaze clashes with his once more, taking in the deep blush that sits high on his cheeks.

"Why are you naked?" I question, my voice husky with need.

When did I become this wanton creature? I've never wanted to climb a man like he's a damn tree but that's all I want to do right now. Or maybe fall to my knees and beg him to fuck my face.

"I can explain," he says but his words are muffled.

In the background a noise continues to interrupt my dream. I don't know what is happening as he slowly starts to fade from my view, his voice drifting off. I can't hear what he is saying and as I try to reach for him, he is gone.

Sitting upright, I take in the apartment around me as the sun starts to rise, light streaming in through the windows, and once more I am bereft at the loss of a man whose damn name I don't even know. How can it hurt so much to lose someone I never even had?

My hormones are still running rampant, and I know I won't be able to concentrate on anything else until I orgasm. Reaching over to the bedside table, I remove my neon green vibrator, switch it to high, and lie back down.

VOLUME ONE

Chapter Six

Korvin Slater

Exploring

For the first time in my life, my animal is quiet. He is there, I can feel him moving around in the recesses of my mind, but he isn't fighting me for dominance or trying to force me to shift. I think it may be because I finally have a plan to talk to our mate. I just need to wait for her to come out of her apartment.

Less than three hours ago, the scent of her pussy, her arousal, permeated the entire building, nearly taking me to my knees. Knowing she is here, close enough to touch, has me making rash decisions, but I can't hold back. And to be honest, I don't want to.

After taking care of my raging erection, again, I showered, dressed, and now I find myself waiting downstairs outside the apartment building for her to emerge. I don't know if she will want to leave her apartment today, having worked late at The Gin Room, but I will wait all day if I have to.

As luck would have it, I don't have to. I've only been loitering outside like a weirdo for twenty minutes when she walks out. Her face is tilted to the sky like she is catching the rays of the sun like a sunflower. Her skin shimmers beneath the rays, begging me to touch her while her red curls bounce in the late morning breeze. For the longest moment I just stare at her.

She turns toward me and freezes. A small smile plays at the corner of her lips as she takes me in.

"Hello."

"Hi." I feel stupid the moment the word falls from

my lips, but I don't know what else to say.

"We haven't been introduced yet," she says, holding out her hand. "I'm Akasha."

I take her hand in mine, feeling her silky skin for the first time. A frisson of awareness runs through me the moment our skin contacts hers.

"Korvin."

She nods, looking at her feet. "I saw you at The Gin Room last night. Do you work there?"

"You could say that."

"Well, I won't keep you. I'm just going in search of some coffee." She tries to pull her hand away, but I hold tight.

"I know a place that has the best coffee. If you don't mind the company," I add on.

"I would love someone who could show me around," she says, a slight blush tinting her cheeks. "I've never been to the city before."

Pride surges through me at the fact she has chosen to spend time with me, allowing me to be her guide. I get to not only spend time with her but show her all my favorite places and keep her safe.

"Let's get you some coffee and then I'll show you around the borough."

****

I spend the entire day with Akasha.

The original plan was only to introduce myself to her but that went out the window quickly, and suddenly I found myself exploring the area I have been living in for the better part of ten years, experiencing everything like it's the first time all over again.

After grabbing coffee, we walk the streets, looking in through shop fronts, eat steak burritos from a street vendor, and even visit the Brooklyn Botanical Gardens. I keep waiting for her to complain that her feet hurt from all the walking, but more often she is the one dragging me behind her to see the next thing.

With every step we take, we talk. I can't remember ever having spoken this much in my life but for some reason it simply flows between us. From where we grew up, childhood memories, favorite colors, and music, to everything in between. Neither of us turn the conversation to anything heavy, but we get to know one another throughout the day.

Her laughter is infectious, and I find myself smiling more often. Another thing I'm not used to. So much that my cheeks hurt from using the muscles.

"Will you look at the time!" she exclaims as she stares at the screen of her cell phone. "We'll have to catch a cab back."

I whistle loudly, holding my hand out to get us a ride. My heart thunders in my chest as we ride back to our building in silence, my large hand still wrapped around her smaller one. I want to say something, to tell her I would like to do this again, but I can't find the words. I feel like after all the talking I've done today, I've simply run out of words.

She smiles at me after we step out of the car, and I pay.

"Thank you, Korvin. I really enjoyed today."

"I'm happy to hear that. I haven't had this much fun in ages," I say with a grin I couldn't hide even if I wanted to.

"Can I tell you something?" she asks shyly.

"Anything."

"Since the moment I got to the city, to Brooklyn, I knew I was meant to be here." I can hear she is trying to explain something but not telling me everything. "I feel like I've known you my entire life."

Leaning down, I kiss her forehead. "Sweet girl, that is the best thing I've heard in ages."

"Really?" she asks, smiling up at me and I wink at her.

"Let's get ready to go to work," I say, cutting into the moment but knowing it needs to be done. For the first time today, my bear rumbles, unhappy with the fact I am halting our progress. "If you want, I can always show you around more another time."

"Oh, I would love to see the catacombs. I read they do a candlelight tour," she says excitedly as we get onto the elevator.

"We'll have to do that tomorrow night, when we're off," I say pressing the button for my floor.

She doesn't select a different floor, and it hits me. We are living beside each other, that's why I could smell her so clearly. She is my new neighbor. The apartment had been sitting vacant for over a year until just this week. Now I know who moved in.

"It's a date," she replies, kissing my cheek and skipping off the elevator to her apartment before disappearing inside.

Chapter Seven

Akasha LaVey

Work, Work, Work

It's been a week since I moved to the city, and I can honestly say I haven't regretted a single moment. I spend my time either working or exploring with Korvin. He shows me his favorite places and we discover new ones together.

The Gin Room is always filled with new and interesting characters, and I quickly make a few new friends.

"Hey, girlie," Ari says as she hops onto the bar.

I smile brightly. "Hey. What have you been up to?"

"Just running some errands for the boss," she says pointing at the floor above us. "You?"

"Not much, just some exploring."

I leave out the part about doing this with Korvin. I have a feeling he wouldn't want people knowing his business. He hasn't said anything to me, but I have learned to trust my gut feelings a long time ago.

"I hope you are enjoying the city," she says with a smile. "I wanted to show you around, but things have been a little hectic."

She blushes and I feel a strange wave of affection for her.

"Don't worry about it," I say, patting her knee. "I am seeing tons of stuff. But maybe we can get together for a movie or a girls' night?"

"Heck, yes!" she exclaims. "We are both off tomorrow night. Let's go have some fun."

I laugh at her enthusiasm. "Sounds like a plan to me."

Ari disappears into the back grabbing some extra glasses for the bar as we finish setting up. Slowly people start trickling in.

"You're new," a voice says behind me as I grab a beer for someone down the bar.

I stare at the man before me. Tall and athletic, dressed in a black suit with a blood red tie, dark hair, sharp features, and an air of danger. To be honest, he is also starkly beautiful, and I can't help but stare.

"Malichai!" Ari calls out from her end. "Stop picking on the staff."

"Ari," he purrs, turning his dark gaze on her. "When will you give in and let me be your man?"

She sneers at the cover model in front of me. "When hell freezes over."

He laughs with his head thrown back. All the while I am trying to figure what the hell is going on. I'm not sure how I feel about my only acquaintance disliking this man so much. Her entire demeanor has changed, the air around her charged with something I can't quite put my finger on. Turning my attention back to him, I wait.

"Don't judge me on Ari's reaction," he says softly. "But know that I messed up and her anger is righteous."

He looks sad as the words fall from his lips and I can't help but wonder what happened. "What can I get you?"

"Vodka rocks."

It takes me a moment to get his order. Once I return, I see the longing in his eyes as he tracks every move she makes.

"Have you tried talking to her?" I ask, leaning closer.

"We are too different. Things were bound to end badly," he says, turning his attention to me. "The worst thing is we both knew it was a bad idea and went ahead with it anyway."

"The heart wants what the heart wants," I say with a small smile, meaning every word.

My thoughts turn to Korvin, and I know he is the man I want.

"Yeah, Doll. But sometimes love isn't enough to overcome the fundamental differences between people."

Malichai drops a bill on the counter before taking his drink and moving into the throng of people. I want to call him back and talk some more, but my attention is drawn to the longing scrolled across my friend's features. My heart hurts for her but I don't know either of them well enough to meddle in their affairs.

Maybe we can talk about it tomorrow night.

****

Just like every night, the hours pass in a blur. "Last round" has been called and only a few stragglers remain inside The Gin Room, finishing off their drinks before they will make their way through the city that never sleeps.

Korvin stands in one of the corners, watching over the entire place. He frowns when another man approaches me, even if it is just to order a drink, and looks like he might hit someone if they stand around making small talk too long. But he doesn't move.

Ari never introduced me to him, so I didn't catch his job description, but I assume he is one of the bouncers or some other form of security. His size alone is enough to intimidate most people, and no one dares to approach his scowling form. He is such a sweetheart when it's just the two of us but has put off heavy "fuck around and find out" vibes once other people are around.

A scuffle breaks out, drawing my attention away from him. At the door, one of the twins—I still can't tell them apart—is holding a man by his throat, his frame pressed against the wall.

"We don't hurt women!" he roars.

I watch his face shimmer and distort, and I swear I see a bull. But the image is gone in seconds. Korvin is beside him, whispering in his ear. Slowly he releases the man before making his way to his brother where a short but curvy woman is wrapped in his arms.

"Akasha." Turning to the unknown voice I stare at the man before me. I know him from my interviews. He is Aldron, the owner of The Gin Room, and my boss. "I need to see you in my office when you're done. And bring Korvin with you. The grumpy old bear should be present for this conversation."

I want to laugh at his description of the man I am quickly falling in love with, but I don't. For some reason I feel trepidation, like a child being called to the headmaster's office. I wonder what he could want to discuss with me, but I have a feeling this could change everything.

Chapter Eight

Korvin Slater

The Box

"Aldron wants to see us," Akasha says as she walks up to me.

Deep inside, my bear bristles. He has been on edge all night, wanting to rip every male in this building limb from limb. Any and every man that has passed through The Gin Room tonight should thank whatever deity they pray to that they are still alive. If I wasn't terrified of scaring Akasha, I would have gone on a rampage tonight.

"Okay." I don't know what else to say.

"You'll have to lead the way," she says, looking at her feet. "I don't know where his office is."

Nodding, I lead her to the elevator, pushing the button for the seventh floor. Aldron may live in the penthouse, but he doesn't conduct business in his home. For a moment we travel in silence but the sound of metal scraping on metal cuts through. With a shudder the elevator comes to a complete standstill, the lights flickering off before the emergency light kicks in.

Akasha grabs my arm, clinging to me. Slowly, I disentangle us before pulling her against my side.

"Don't worry. It's an old building," I say, pressing the alarm button. "It's probably just a power outage."

"Okay," she replies. There is a tremble in her voice, and I wish I could say something more reassuring. "I'm just happy you're here. I wouldn't be able to handle this alone."

I gently cup her face, tilting her chin up so I can look at her. In her tear-filled gaze, I see nothing but trust. For long moments we simply stare at one another, the stress of being stuck in an elevator completely forgotten.

"Are you going to kiss me now?" she whispers, licking her lips.

I thought I was in control. I was under the illusion that I could spend time with her, protect her, without being affected by her presence.

I was wrong.

Pressing my lips against hers is the biggest mistake I could have made. It is also the greatest moment of my long, lonely life. She sighs, wrapping her arms around my neck and standing on her toes. Her curvy body presses against mine and any control I had slips into oblivion.

I push her back against the wall as my tongue licks at the seam of her lips, they part instantly, allowing me access. Her taste explodes across my senses and my bear purrs like a fucking cat. It's something he has never done but I know he is happy. My bear and I are finally on the same fucking page and the violence that has ruled our lives for so many years falls away.

My hands mold to Akasha's ass as her finger plays through my hair. A moan falls from her lips as she throws her head back. Lifting her up, she wraps her legs around my middle and my lips find the smooth caramel skin of her neck. Kissing, licking, and nipping, I taste her all over, like a man possessed.

"Korvin," she says breathily.

"Yes, my sweet," I reply against her neck.

"Please," she begs sweetly.

I know what she wants. I can smell her arousal. It permeates every corner of the small metal box we are trapped in and fills every crack in my damaged soul, imprinting her on me for the rest of my life. I knew the mate bond would be potent, but I haven't even claimed her yet and I already know I would die without her.

"Not here," I say, pressing my forehead to hers. "I don't want to claim you in a damn elevator."

"Please," she begs again.

"I'll make you a deal," I say, knowing I am pushing my boundaries and testing the control I have over my bear. "I'll make you come on my fingers and when we get home, I'll fuck you till you can't walk."

I let my dirty words hang between us. I have been fighting the need to claim her because I was afraid of what my bear would do, terrified he would hurt her. But if these past few days have taught me anything, it's that she soothes my beast. My bear has never been more docile or manageable than when she is beside me.

Akasha stares at me for long moments before she speaks, her words a whisper for my ears only. "Do you promise?"

I kiss her in reply, ravaging her mouth.

When I saw her for the first time tonight, I almost lost my shit. She was wearing a plaid black skirt instead of her customary skinny jeans, putting her tone legs on display for the entire world. Jealousy thrummed through me and my bear roared in outrage, rattling my brain around in my skull. But now I couldn't be more thankful for the easy access.

My cock throbs painfully in the confines of my dark blue jeans as pre-cum slips down my shaft but any pain is worth having her in my arms. Slowly, I lower her body down mine, until her feet are on the ground. My right hand releases her full ass cheek to slip beneath the fabric of her skirt and caress the skin of her thigh, working its way around to the front.

A groan falls from my lips when I don't encounter

any resistance.

"Why aren't you wearing any panties?" I ask, my voice low and rough. "Are you trying to get fucked?"

"Yes, Korvin," she replies.

I harshly shove a finger into her dripping channel. The sound that falls from her lips nearly takes me out at the knees but the irrational anger swimming through my veins keeps me standing.

"So, you just want to get laid?" I ask angrily, rousing my bear from his contentment. "Any cock will do?"

She moans like a fucking whore and the sound makes my cock jerk against the zipper of my jeans. With every spear of my fingers, she works her little pussy against my hand.

"No!" she moans loudly. "You. Your cock."

The anger drains from me instantly knowing she was hoping to either seduce or entice me.

"Fuck, woman. The thought of you with another man … I'll kill any other man that comes near what is mine."

"Yours." The word is a broken whisper as my thumb finds her clit, rubbing in circles.

"You're stunning," I whisper in her ear. I need to give her praise after my unfounded accusation a moment ago, all while continuing to work her over with my fingers. "Your pussy is so wet. No idea how I am going to get my fat cock in this tiny little hole."

"Oh, God." She throws her head back in pleasure, spreading her thighs even more for me.

"Show me your tits, Sweetness," I beg this time, needing to see more of her.

Yes, we are stuck in an elevator, and it could start moving any second but neither of us care right now. We are both lost in the moment.

Akasha does as I ask, undoing the buttons on the short-sleeve black jacket before undoing the buttons on the shirt. The fabric falls to the side, showing me the black lace that holds her large breasts in place. I can't resist pulling one of the cups down, baring her dark nipple to my gaze.

My lips wrap around the turgid tip, sucking harshly. Akasha screams loud and long as her pussy grips my fingers, her orgasm pulling her under. My fingers continue the ministrations through the aftershocks until the last of her pleasure has passed.

"Fuck me, that was sexy," I say, slipping my fingers from her sopping pussy and licking them off.

She watches every move I make. She grabs my hand and sucks my thumb into her mouth, licking her own juices off the digit, and I swear I almost come in my jeans. I want to tell her how fucking exquisite she is, how desperate I am to be inside her, that I love her, but the lights flicker and soon the elevator is moving.

I quickly help her fix her clothing before we arrive on the seventh floor.

Chapter Nine

Akasha LaVey

Secrets

My legs feel like jelly as I walk beside Korvin. I have just had the single best sexual experience in my fucking life and now I have to talk to my damn boss.

All I want to do is catch a cab home and let Korvin fulfill his dirty promise of fucking me until I can't walk. I don't even care that I have plans with Ari tomorrow, I'll tell her I'm sick or something. Yes, it is a dick move but if I have to wake up from another erotic fucking dream featuring Korvin and what I can only imagine will be a spectacular cock, I'll jump out my apartment window. It's the same reason I didn't wear panties tonight.

I was hoping I could somehow seduce him. Get him to touch me, kiss me, fuck me. It's like a living entity, this need to be taken by him. I don't want sweet and soft, I want him to treat me like a possession to take what he needs and leave me in a sobbing, messy heap of sexual satisfaction.

Each moment I spend with him only makes the desire within me grow more. I know what I am feeling isn't normal by any stretch of the word, but I don't want to give up on what he makes me feel. I crave him more every day.

Korvin knocks on the ornately carved wooden door and waits, my hand in his.

"Enter." Both of us step inside. "Please take a seat," Aldron says. He gestures to the two black leather chairs in front of his desk.

I wish Korvin would pull me down on his lap so I could feel his erection against my ass, but I know he won't. Besides, that would be even more inappropriate than what we did in the elevator. I mean, this is our boss's office.

"You wanted to see us?" Korvin asks.

Aldron nods. "This is not quite how I intended to do this, but things have happened, and I need to move up my timeline."

"Okay," I say with a raised brow, unsure of what they are talking about.

"This is all going to seem a bit crazy, but I need you to listen to me—" Aldron starts, facing me but Korvin cuts him off.

"Hell, no!" he roars, standing upright, shaking the windows in their panes. "You will not tell her anything."

Like before with one of our bouncer twins, his features shimmer and shift before returning to normal. I shake my head. Being overly tired, hopped up on energy drinks, and sex deprived is making me hallucinate.

"Sit. Down," Aldron orders Korvin. The strange thing is he does what he is told. "Akasha, do me a favor and sit on his lap."

"What?"

"It will keep him in his seat," he replies with a shrug.

I don't argue, instead doing what I wanted to do from the beginning and taking a seat on Korvin's lap. My ass wriggles against his erection and he wraps one of his muscular arms around my middle to keep me from squirming.

"Please Aldron, don't do this." Korvin is pleading with Aldron, and I don't understand why.

"It needs to be done. The situation has ... changed."

"Can someone please tell me what the hell is going on?"

Korvin sighs. "You need to listen to Aldron and keep an open mind. Afterward, we can talk."

The tone of his voice and the way he is holding me right now speaks volumes. He thinks whatever Aldron must tell me will either piss me off or send me running. He doesn't believe there will be an opportunity for us to talk. He thinks I won't want to.

I fully intend to prove him wrong. Korvin doesn't know this about me, but I am stubborn as fuck. And I want him, so I won't be backing off anytime soon. Well, maybe if Aldron tells me he is a mass murdering cannibal, but even then, I'm not sure I would walk away.

"You didn't get this job by chance. You were vetted and found to be the strongest candidate for what we needed."

"Anyone can bartend," I say with a roll of my eyes.

Aldron chuckles. "That is true. But that's not why you're here." I am confused beyond measure. So instead of speaking, I wait for him to continue. "Everything I have created in the last three hundred years is under threat. No one respects the old ways anymore and they are trying to work me out."

"Three hundred years?" I ask incredulously.

"Let me start at the beginning. I am a vampire." He flashes a set of distended fangs at me, his eyes glowing an eerie yellow. "And you are a witch."

"Excuse me?" I squeak.

My mind is still reeling from the vampire bit and now he is telling me I'm not what I thought I was. Korvin rubs his fingers across the exposed sliver of flesh between my skirt and shirt.

"You are a direct descendant of the witch, Marie

Laveau. After the accusations in New Orleans, your forefathers must have changed your last name to escape the stigma that came with being part of the Laveau line."

"My grandmother told me the stories when I was a child," I muse softly.

"So, you know?" Korvin asks.

"They were the ramblings of a crazy old lady," I say. But deep down inside I know she wasn't crazy, no matter what my mother used to say.

"You know you don't believe that no matter what you say," Aldron says with confidence. "You've always felt outside of everyone and everything else, like you don't fit in or belong anywhere. Strange things have happened around you for your entire life, and you probably have some kind of visions or premonitions."

"How do you know that?"

"Because all witches are the same with the basics," he replies. "What matters are the natural abilities. Like your healing power."

"What?"

"The way you healed the woman's hand on your first night here was amazing."

"I didn't…"

"You did. And even though you weren't raised as a witch, your latent abilities make you the perfect candidate for what I need."

"Just get to the point, Aldron," Korvin says gruffly.

"I want you to study with some of the local witches. We need someone powerful enough to cast a protection spell around Brooklyn to keep Lucius from getting in and taking over," he explains. "He is pure anarchy and chaos."

"Meaning?" I ask.

"My brother doesn't believe in the sanctity of life

and inner species living. Where I prefer to find donors to fulfill my dietary needs, he will bring his coven here and they will destroy the harmony we have created. No human, shifter, magical being, or even animal will be safe from them. And then he will move on and destroy the next place."

"Shifters? Magical creatures?" My mind is swirling with everything he is telling me.

"If witches are real, won't so much more be true also?"

"I think that's enough for now," Korvin cut in. "Why don't you give her a chance to process everything, and she can come to you if and when she is ready?"

"Korvin," Aldron starts but stops abruptly.

"It is not your story to tell." Korvin's tone is final as he stands placing me on my feet. "Let's get you home, Akasha."

VOLUME ONE

Chapter Ten

Korvin Slater

The Forest

The drive from The Gin Room is quiet and intense for longer than I am comfortable. I know Aldron has shocked her with everything he said. She is working through a million things right now.

"What else do I need to know about?" Akasha asks softly, gazing out into the rainy night through the passenger side window.

"So much."

She sighs and I know that no matter the outcome, I cannot keep hiding my true self from her. Instead of continuing back to the apartment building where we both live, I turn us in the direction of the small forest I frequent for my shifts.

"Where are we...?"

"I'm going to show you everything. My entire truth," I explain.

"You don't have to."

"I want to. You deserve to know who I really am before we go any further with whatever this is between us," I say, knowing full well this could be the thing that sends her screaming in another direction. "I'm also tired of hiding," I add honestly.

She nods, her gaze locked on the side of my face as I drive. Nerves thrum through me as I drive us through the darkened city covered in its sheet of rain. The moment my truck stops in the parking lot I know I have run out of time. Climbing out of the truck, I make my way to her side, my hand trembling as I open the door for her to get out.

"I don't have an umbrella," I say softly as she stands before me in the light mist of rain.

"It's fine," she says cupping my jaw and forcing me to look at her. "I don't mind the rain."

With a nod, I take her hand in mine and lead her down the muddy path into the heart of the small forest. My nerves are getting the better of me and for the longest moment I fully consider turning the fuck around and just going home so I can sleep.

But I know this is one of those moments that needs to be faced head on. Either way this is going to change my life forever.

Stopping, I take Akasha's face in my hands. Gently I kiss her lips for what may be the last time in my life.

"No matter what happens after this," I say once I pull away from her. "Know that no matter what you decide, my feelings for you will remain the same."

"Korvin?"

"Just give me a minute."

I take my time stripping out of my clothes. Whether she leaves or not, I can't go running around Brooklyn naked. I fold my clothes and set them on a rock, turning to look at her for one last time.

Taking a deep breath, I call my bear forward, allowing the shift to come over me. The shimmer of the magic distorts the vision of her in front of me until I am fully in my animal form. The two of us stare at each other for the longest moment.

"You're a bear." The words are breathed out of her, a sigh on the wind as she steps closer.

I shake my head, discouraging her from coming any closer. I don't know how my bear will react, and my fear keeps me back even in this moment where it doesn't seem she has an ounce of fear.

"Now everything makes sense, "she says, laughing loudly. "I've been dreaming of you for so long. Not just you, Korvin, but your animal too."

I didn't realize how close she was until I felt her fingers brush through the fur on my chest. My bear sits perfectly still, allowing her to touch him, once more purring like a cat. He is content, happy to let her pay him attention.

"Is this what you were holding back from me? Is this what you thought would make me see you differently?"

My bear grunts, making her laugh again.

"Okay, big buy," she says, scratching beneath my bear's chin. "I need to talk to Korvin."

He snorts and shakes his head.

"Don't be that way," she says and chuckles. "I promise to make him let you out more. I have a feeling he hasn't been letting you have the spotlight often."

My bear grumbles but allows me to shift back. Akasha smiles at me with a fondness I never expected from her, especially not after meeting my bear.

"After I met you the first time, I dreamed of a big black bear. He led me through a meadow," she explains her dream to me not knowing I had the exact same one. "You were there, angry that I had followed him. Now I know why. You're afraid of your animal."

I smile. "I'm not afraid of him. I'm afraid of what he is capable of."

"He seems sweet to me."

"Yeah, well. There is a first time for everything," I say with a chuckle.

"I think I am meant to be here, that I was meant to meet you."

"There is one more thing you need to know," I

say softly, grabbing my jeans and slipping them up my legs. "Shifters … we mate for life."

"Mate?"

I blush for the first time since we met each other. I mean, she just saw me naked and this is the thing that makes me blush.

"Each shifter has a fated mate, a soulmate, so to speak. At eighteen we can find our fated mates. Some find them quickly, some search for years, and some never find their other half. You are my mate."

She stares at me in disbelief. "Is that why I have been dreaming of you?"

"We have been dreaming of each other."

"Really?" She frowns.

"I have been dreaming of you for more than six months. I didn't know how to find you or where to start looking. It was driving me crazy," I explain. I take her hand now that I am fully dressed and lead her back to the truck.

"What does that mean?" she asks as I help her into the truck.

"It means I belong to you. Mind, heart, and soul," I say once I join her inside the cab.

Chapter Eleven

Akasha LaVey

What I Want

The drive back to the apartment building is long and tense. I have a million more questions I want to ask, but I'm not sure Korvin is in the right headspace at the moment. I want to know about his bear, about other shifters, about Aldron and the coming danger he spoke of. But most of all, I want to know about fated mates and what that means for us.

Korvin parks the truck in the basement and leads me to the elevator. The air between us feels charged, especially remembering what he did to me mere hours ago in a metal box just like this one. The memory alone is enough to have arousal thrumming through my veins once more.

When the elevator door slides open, we both step out.

"You have a lot to think about," Korvin says, his gaze locked somewhere over my head. "And some hard decisions to make."

"Korvin..."

"Take the night, Akasha," he cuts in. "Get some rest. The shock hasn't hit you yet, you are taking this much too calmly. We can talk in the morning if you want."

I want to argue with him, tell him he doesn't know what I can handle or what I want, but he is already gone. The door to his apartment is closed and I hear the lock click in place.

How fucking dare he make decisions for me?

Slamming the door to my own apartment I stomp through my living space, wearing my anger like a cloak. It takes me a moment to realize that my cell phone is ringing and another to dig it out of my handbag. I stare at the screen, not sure if I should answer or not, but I do need someone to talk to.

"Ari…"

"Can I come to you? We need to talk. I can't believe Aldron talked to you without me." Her words are going a mile a minute and I can't even get in a word edgewise. "I should have smacked that smug smirk off his handsome face."

"Ari!" I all but shout to get her attention. When she finally stays quiet, I talk again. "Please…" but the word gets caught on a sob.

"Open the door."

I stumble to the door, opening it to find the only friend I have standing there. I didn't even realize I was full-on crying until she wrapped her arms around me, closing the door and leading me to the couch.

"Hush now. Everything will be all right."

I shake my head vehemently, swiping angrily at my tears. I want to scream at the injustice of the moment, but I can't stop sobbing.

"Why don't you take a deep breath and tell me what is going on? Aldron said you were okay when you left his office," she says rubbing soothing circles on my back.

I take a few deep breaths with my eyes closed trying to calm and center myself. I can't very well get any advice if she doesn't know what's going on. When I finally have myself under control, I pull my legs up beneath me and focus on Ari.

"I can deal with what Aldron told me. I have always been resilient and quick to adapt to change. I'm not sure how I feel about being the great witchy hope, but it doesn't seem like I have much choice in the situation. I won't allow vampires to overrun Brooklyn and hurt innocent people."

"That's very … pragmatic," she says with a frown.

"Probably."

"So why the tears?"

"It's Korvin."

"Fuck me," she mumbles, running her hand through her brightly colored hair. "What did he do this time?"

I want to laugh at her reaction but all I can do is give her a small, sad smile. "It's a long story but suffice it to say he thinks I can't handle everything that's going on."

"Did he tell you about his bear?"

"He showed me."

The shock on her face is so comical I can't help but giggle.

"That's a big step for a shifter, especially Korvin," she explains. "Humans rarely react well to finding they're not alone in the world, not to mention that they aren't at the top of the food chain."

"It doesn't bother me. I've been dreaming of him and his bear for a long time." She gasps, covering her mouth with her hand so I just blurt out everything else. "He says I'm his fated mate. But now he's shut me out and I honestly don't know what to do."

Ari claps her hands excitedly. "I knew there was something going on."

"There's nothing going on," I say, sulking like a six-year-old who didn't get their way. "We were all hot and heavy and then he shut me out completely."

"He's trying to protect you. It's what male shifters

do," she explains, a tinge of sadness in her voice. "They would rather be unhappy but know you're not sad or hurt."

"That is such bullshit!"

"Believe me, I know … how do you feel about using your feminine wiles to get the man you want? You do want him, right?"

"More than my next breath," I confess softly. "I was half in love with him before I even met him, and now I'm lost to him."

"Perfect. Then this is what you're going to do."

Chapter Twelve

Korvin Slater

Toys? Not on my Watch

She slams the door to her apartment, and I want to put my fist through a wall. I listen to her move around and all I want to do is go to her. Her phone rings and the sob she releases tears my soul to shreds. I hear Ari next door, and I hope she can offer my mate some support.

My bear whimpers—for the first time in his damn life—while she cries, and it takes everything I have in me to stay in my own apartment. Instead of going to the woman I love and claiming her like I want, I strip down and get in the shower.

After cleaning myself thoroughly, I shut off the water, dry myself with one of the dark grey towels, and fall into bed naked. All I want to do is sleep this fucking night away and hope things look better in the morning.

I lay there taking in the silence when a noise catches my attention. First, I think Akasha is crying again but then I recognize it for what it really is. A moan.

My senses are on full alert and a moment later I can smell her arousal through the walls. I know I have no right to wonder what she is doing, but my mind is flooded with erotic visions of my sexy mate spread out across her bed.

I listen intently to the sounds she makes, the slight sound of her vibrator playing in the background, and I grind my teeth. I should be the one to bring her pleasure, not a battery-operated toy. But I will stay away and give her space.

Instead, I wrap my hand around my painful

erection and stroke myself while listening to her pleasure herself.

"Korvin."

Her moan is loud and the word rattles around inside my mind, rousing my sulking bear. Within the blink of an eye, I am out of bed and pulling on a pair of sweats. I will break the fucking door down to get to her if I have to. Knowing she is right next door fucking herself with a toy and my name on her lips has the last vestiges of decency falling away. If she can still think of me in a sexual way, she clearly hasn't been scared off.

I stomp from my apartment to hers, intending to pound my fist on her door before I kick it in. But there is no need for that. The moment I reach her threshold I can see a sliver of light from inside, her door not properly closed. I push it open slowly, scenting the air and tasting her arousal. I close the door behind me and make sure the lock is engaged before making my way through her apartment to where I know her bedroom is located.

I watch her in the lamplight, gloriously naked for me to devour with my gaze. She has a pink toy in her right hand that she slowly fucks into her pussy. Her eyes are closed, head thrown back, passionate moans falling from her lips. I can't help but run a hand over my painful erection as I trace every curve of her body.

"Korvin," she moans again. "Please fuck me. Make me yours."

Her words snap me out of my stupor, and I walk into her bedroom without her permission. I harshly grab her ankles and pull her to the edge of the bed.

Akasha looks at me with a hooded gaze, a sultry smile on her lips. "Took you long enough," she whispers.

My gaze is locked on her pussy where the pink vibrator continues to do its dance. It's both hot as fuck to see and offensive to me. She will never be able to replace me with a mere toy.

"Take the toy out," I say, my voice low enough to almost be a growl. My bear prowling in the corners of my mind.

"Why?" her voice is sultry, talking directly to my throbbing cock. "I'm so close to coming."

She cups her breasts, tweaking at the dusky nipples, and I want to roar. "You should come riding my tongue."

She spreads her thighs wider with a moan, her hips tilting up into the air. "If you want me, you'll have to take me. I'm tired of throwing myself at you."

I don't wait for her to say any more. I rip the offensive toy from her channel and throw it hard enough against the wall that it breaks in two. I hear her harsh inhale, but I'm not concerned with her broken toy, or the divot that will surely be in the wall. I'm only thinking of her taste.

Pulling her ass to the edge of the bed, I fall to my knees and lick her slit like it's an ice cream. The moment I suck her hardened clit into my mouth she goes off like a fucking rocket. Her thighs tremble as she screams my name. My cock kicks in my sweats, begging to be set free while pre-cum slips from the crown and down the length.

I continue to lick and suck at her pussy as she shakes through the most amazing orgasm I have ever seen.

"Please," Akasha begs in a broken whisper.

"Baby," I say holding my body over hers. "You need to be sure."

"I am sure," she says, cupping my face.

"If you let me fuck you tonight there will be no going back," I explain as I nuzzle into her palm. "I will breed you, mark you, and claim you."

"Yes!" she moans, rubbing her sex against my

covered cock. "I want to be yours. Forever."

I flip her over on her stomach, pushing her knees beneath her body. Her chest is pressed flat to the bed and her pussy is dripping wet. The sight before me is dirty and erotic and I've never seen anything as beautiful in my entire life. My bear purrs in agreement while my little mate wriggles her ass.

"Stay still," I command, slapping her right ass cheek.

A sharp intake of breath is followed by a moan before she moves once more.

"I'm serious, Akasha," I say, slapping her again. "I need to take my time, or I could hurt you."

She stops her wriggling but opens her legs wider beneath her weight, offering herself to me. She has no idea what she is doing to me in this moment. Dropping my sweats I hold my pre-cum slicked cock in my hand, slowly rubbing the head through her folds. It's like liquid fire against the crown of my erection and I know I will never be the same again after this.

The crown bumps against her clit and she hisses. The sound goes straight to my balls, and I notch my cock at her entrance before slowly feeding an inch into her channel.

"Fuck," I moan. "You're so tight."

"Yes," she moans beneath me, clawing at her bedding.

"Stay still, woman. I want to make it all the way inside you before I paint your womb with my cum."

"Fuck," she moans. "Why is that so fucking hot?"

"What, Baby?" I push another inch deeper, taking my time and torturing us both as I watch my cock disappear inside her.

"Fucking you raw." She looks at me over her shoulder. "Knowing you will come inside me and it will drip out afterward."

"Fuck!" I thrust all the way inside her, no longer able to hold back.

A second orgasm crashes over her, her walls massaging my length and trying to pull the cum right out of me. Her scream is loud enough I'm sure the entire fucking building just heard her, but I don't care.

Taking hold of her hips, I withdraw before thrusting into her harshly over and over. My bear is losing his mind, roaring so loudly I'm afraid I'll go deaf. But I don't stop. My mate moans, tearing at the sheets, pushing her ass back into every thrust. I smack her ass cheek for a third time and her pussy contracts, strangling my cock.

"Yes, Baby," I say brokenly, watching my cock slip in and out of her. "Fuck this fat cock, milk me, take my cum."

"Korvin, please," she pleads. "I need more."

"I know what you need, little witch."

Grabbing her hair, I pull her body up against mine, her back to my front. I kiss and lick the column of her neck while my other hand harshly tweaks her nipple. I can feel the flutter of her pussy start once more signaling her orgasm is getting close.

"You're mine now," I whisper in her ear. "Mine to cherish. To love. To fuck. To breed."

My teeth sink into her skin just above her clavicle, drawing blood and marking her. The room glows with a purple haze as she comes hard on my cock, dragging me into bliss with her. I come like I never have before, my vision going blurry.

The moment I let her go, she falls onto the bed, completely spent. The purple haze that lightened the room moments ago clings to her skin and I know her magic and mine are bound forever.

Slowly I start to move my hips once more, my cock still fully erect inside her.

"How can you already go again?" she asks breathlessly. "Aren't you an old man?"

I chuckle, thrusting harshly. "Brat." I smack her ass for good measure. "You're mated to a bear now. I can fuck you for hours, through multiple orgasms for both of us."

Chapter Thirteen

Akasha LaVey

Calling for Help

I wake wrapped in thick arms. He is awake, murmuring things to either me or himself. I pretend to be asleep hoping he won't be able to tell the difference. My body is deliciously sore in all the right places and like a bitch in heat, I want to present myself to him for a fresh round of fucking.

"Behave yourself, Korvin," he admonishes in a whisper. "Let her rest. You've claimed her, she is yours forever."

I feel his hand caress my ass before slipping between my legs. Slowly he pushes a single finger inside me. I fight not to move or moan.

"So wet and slippery. I'll try not to wake her."

He is clearly talking to himself. Slowly he removes his hand and lifts my thigh over his hip. His hard cock slides into me without any resistance and I bite my lip to hold my moan. He thinks I'm sleeping. He wants me enough to fuck my sleeping form. The thought is enough to have a moan escaping.

"Shit." He stops moving and I want to cry. "I didn't mean to wake you."

"That much is apparent," I say with a giggle. "But I'm awake now."

****

We spend four days in my apartment. Korvin explains that this is the most important time in a newly mated couples' relationship. It's where they strengthen their bond.

But no one can live in a bubble forever and soon the real world interrupts us. Korvin's cell phone rings just after sunset and I can feel his demeanor change before he answers.

"Aldron."

He listens for a bit before setting the device to "speaker."

"Hello, Akasha," Aldron says. "I'm terribly sorry to bother both of you at this time but we need your help."

"My help?" I ask, confused.

"Could you come down to The Gin Room?"

I look to Korvin, who is already moving around, and he nods. "We're on our way."

Luckily, we had only just gotten out of the shower so we could dress quickly and jump in Korvin's truck. My nerves are frayed as we drive the few blocks to The Gin Room, not knowing what is waiting for us.

"I can feel your trepidation, Mate," Korvin says casually. "But you don't need to worry. Aldron knows you are limited in your powers, and I will be there every step of the way."

I smile at him, thankful for his reassurance as we stop across the street. The Gin Room should already be open and filling up with people. But on the door is a notice:

CLOSED UNTIL FURTHER NOTICE

What the hell is going on here? Korvin knocks and a moment later one of the twins opens the door. His face is ashen, and I can see that something bad has happened.

"Thanks for coming," he says. "They're downstairs."

"What happened?" Korvin asks.

"Knox got into it with a vampire from Arkansas over the weekend. He hit the girl that was with him," he explains as we cross the empty bar and make our way down the stairs. "Turns out she wasn't with him willingly and he was using her as a damn blood bag. We took her home with us."

His ears turn bright red, and I hear Korvin chuckle softly. I must be missing something.

"Anyway, Aldron said with Akasha starting her training, Celeste could have the position at the bar until we figured out what to do. We were opening and getting ready for tonight when the asshole vamp returned with three friends."

"Is Knox hurt?" I ask as we reach the bottom step.

"You could say that."

In front of me is a scene of pure carnage. On every surface of what I assume is an underground fighting ring is blood. There are two dead men lying outside the ring, and Knox is in the center. His head rests on the lap of a pretty blonde woman I have never met but vaguely remember. Beside her is a willowy brunette woman in a flowy emerald green dress. But the thing that grabs my attention is the fact that Knox is basically grey.

I quickly make my way over to them and crouch down, my fingers on the inside of his left wrist, looking for a pulse. Just when I am about to give up, I find it, thready and weak. The blonde woman is sobbing softly, pushing his hair off his forehead and whispering softly to him.

"What can I do?" I ask the other woman.

Her gaze clashes with mine like she is only now realizing she isn't alone anymore. "I need to tap into your natural magic. If my coven was here, I would call on them, but everyone is out of town for the blood moon ceremony."

"Okay," I say instantly, wanting to help before he dies. "You'll need to walk me through this step by step."

She stares at me in disbelief. "Aldron said you were a novice, but you don't know anything, do you?"

"Nope."

"You and I are going to have fun once your training starts," she says with a chuckle. "But for now, let's save Knox. We can chat later."

She takes my right hand in hers and places my right hand on his chest, over his heart, that is barely moving with his labored breaths. It's only then I see the massive hole in his chest.

"We just need to get him back to this side of the living," she explains. "Once he can sit up, he will be able to shift and then he can heal naturally. Close your eyes and clear your mind."

I do as she says but it's harder than one would think.

"Think of fire, the way the flames dance, the way the heat caresses your skin," she whispers.

I feel my fingers tingle, just the way they did the other night in the bar, and then her laughter. I open my eyes to see what has her reacting this way. Our hands are glowing purple, little sparks between our fingers. Beneath my hand, I can feel heat pouring into Knox. Already his color is improving, and he takes a deep breath.

The blonde woman stares at me in fascination as I continue to let the flames consume my mind. A moment later, the hole in his chest starts to heal before my eyes and he coughs. I push harder, trying to give him more of my magic but the woman beside me stops me.

"Enough," she barks. "Never put your own life force at risk." She takes my hand off his chest as Knox starts to sit upright. "He has his own magic that will help him heal."

I nod, watching the man before me. The blonde woman is now full-out sobbing. Cruz wraps her in his arms, moving her out of the way as his twin stands. I watch the magic of the shift flow over him. It looks like he is struggling to shift, and I place my hand on his ankle, giving him just a little more of my magic.

In the next moment, his shift is complete, and I am thrown for a loop. Before me stands a mythical creature. More so than a vampire or a bear shifter. No, he is a fucking Minotaur.

I open my mouth to say something but darkness envelops me.

VOLUME ONE

Chapter Fourteen

Korvin Slater

Aftermath

"What the fuck?" I roar at Krishka as I watch my mate slump into a heap on the mat of the octagon.

She shakes her head with a roll of her eyes. "Will you relax, Bear?" she snaps at me. "Your little witch doesn't take direction well. She depleted her reserves, giving Knox more than she should. Her body needs rest."

I have Akasha swept up into my arms as I glare at her. "How often will this happen?"

"Until she learns her limitations or kills herself. Whichever happens first."

"What can I do?" I feel impotent at this moment.

"Not much," Krishka says. "Make sure she stays hydrated once she wakes up, and talk to her. Not shouty black bear bullshit. Just talk."

I glare at her before moving toward the stairs. Once I emerge into The Gin Room, Aldron stands there waiting for me.

"Take one of the open apartments upstairs," he says. "Taking her all the way back home will be difficult alone. Besides, now that you're mated, I'll want you living here instead, especially with her training."

I nod and make my way to the elevator. Aldron follows us inside, chooses a floor, and leads us to a vacant apartment. He doesn't linger or speak. He simply nods before he closes the door and leaves us alone.

The entire apartment is decorated in white without a single personal touch, a lot like my own apartment. If this is where Akasha and I will be staying for the foreseeable future, I can't wait to see what she will do to make it more a home than just another place to stay.

I lay her down on the stark white bedding and stare at her. What the fuck am I supposed to do until she wakes up?

****

She sleeps for six fucking hours. Six of the longest, most stressful hours of my life. Just when I want to give up and call Krishka to come and check on her, she stirs, her eyes fluttering open. She smiles when she sees me, and I don't know if I want to kiss her or tan her ass.

"How are you feeling?"

"Thirsty." Her voice is hoarse, and I quickly hand her a bottle of cold water.

She scoots around on the bed, resting against the headboard as she slowly sips from the bottle.

"Is this your apartment?" she asks looking around with a frown.

"No. Aldron has been converting one of the floors in the building for the mated couples. The apartments are for single staff."

"Ari didn't mention that. She just said there were apartments and office space," she says, taking in everything around here. "Does that mean we'll be moving?"

"Already moved," I correct. "Aldron had someone pack up our apartments while you were asleep. They just dropped everything here."

"Damn!" She whistled. "That man moves fast. How long was I asleep?"

"Six hours."

"Really? It felt like ten minutes."

"Krishka, the head of the Obsidian Coven, said

you need to rest and this will happen often until you learn to listen." I know I'm frowning but at least my tone is even. I don't want her to feel like a chastised child or that I am fighting with her, but I need her to know how scared I was. "You need to take what Krishka tells you and teaches you to heart, Little Mate."

"I know." She looks at her hands with the water bottle still clutched between her fingers. "I just wanted to help."

"I know, and your heart is one of the reasons I fell in love with you, but you can't put yourself in danger like that. I can't remember ever being that scared in all my forty-five years."

"You love me?" she asks softly, staring at me with wide eyes.

I frown. Surely, I have said the words in the past four days of lovemaking, fucking, and all my efforts to breed her. But I can't think of a single time those words crossed my lips.

I sit beside her on the bed and take her face in my hands. I kiss her, hard, pouring all my love and passion into the single action.

"I love you, Akasha," I say once I pull away. "I love your body and your mind. Your beautiful soul and your open heart. I love the way you say my name in your sleep and the birthmark on your left butt cheek. I love you completely and irrevocably."

A tear slips down her cheek and I gently wipe it away with my thumb.

"And I love you too," she whispers. "You and your beautiful black bear."

VOLUME ONE

Chapter Fifteen

Akasha LaVey

Learning About Myself

After our declaration of love, Korvin slips into bed behind me and cuddles me through the night. it isn't about sex, even though I'm sure both of us would happily fuck each other's brains out. This is about connecting and showing affection without getting naked. Weird concept, I know, but I have never felt so special and cherished in my entire life.

Once we wake to the new day and the bright sunlight coming in through the open drapes, we shower together, taking care to wash each other before getting dirty all over again. Korvin fucks me against the white tiles until I scream, and then we have breakfast.

A knock at the door draws our attention. I lift a brow in his direction.

"I don't know anyone in Brooklyn," I say with a smile. "Must be for you."

He walks toward the door with a grumble. "No one visits me."

"You'll have to get used to visitors," I say with a laugh. "I'm a social person. Maybe it's Ari."

He shakes his head, trying to hide his own smile as he opens the door. His immediate frown lets me know it isn't someone he wants to see.

"What do you want?" he asks right before Krishka, the witch from last night, ducks under his arm.

"Chill out, Grumpa. I'm here to see your witch."

I can't hold in my giggle at her nickname for him, which only earns me a scowl.

"She needs more rest," Korvin says to her.

"She needs to listen, then she won't have to rest," she retorts as she reaches me where I'm drinking my coffee at the breakfast nook. "Besides, we are running out of time. She needs to master her element before I can teach her anything else or she won't be able to control the fire."

"My element?" I ask, intrigued.

"You're a fire witch," she says with a bounce of her eyebrows. "Shifters can smell their mates, I can smell elemental witches."

I wrinkle my nose at her. "So, I smell like smoke?"

She laughs, packing items on the counter she pulls from her shoulder bag. "Not at all. Each elemental witch's scent is unique. Yours is more like s'mores. You know, caramelizing marshmallows."

"That's not so bad."

"It wasn't," she says giving me a side eye. "That is, until you depleted your reserves. "Then it turned to a burnt sugar smell."

"Sorry."

"Don't apologize, I was the same when I first realized my power. But you're still new to all of this," she says motioning with an outstretched arm. "You need to learn how to replenish and use your energy without killing yourself."

Korvin snorts from the doorway.

"I'll be teaching your mate the basics, you're welcome to leave if you won't be supportive," she snaps.

"Witch, don't start…"

"Stop!" I cut in. "I don't know what it is with the two of you, but cut it out! You're giving me a headache." Both look chastised so I continue. "Korvin, please go do some shopping. We have nothing except coffee in this place."

He gives me a dubious look and I smile in return.

"I promise to listen to Krishka and not overexert myself. And you'll only be gone for an hour so you can check on me when you get back."

"Fine," he grumbles once more. "But I will be more than grumpy if something happens to you while I'm gone."

"O ye of little faith," I say kissing him on the lips as he walks past us. "Nothing is going to happen to me."

He closes the bathroom door to get dressed and I offer Krishka some coffee. I've barely handed her the mug when he walks back out. Dressed in dark blue jeans and a dark green t-shirt, he looks good enough to eat. He grabs his keys and wallet off the counter before kissing me passionately and then walking out the door. I know he won't be gone for long. It's not in his nature to stay away from me.

With a blush I turn to the other witch. "What are we doing?"

She rubs her hands together. "I'm going to teach you basic spells. Each day we will practice something new until you are ready to cast the protection spell we need. Don't worry, you won't cast that big a spell alone, my coven is just too small to do it on our own."

"How many people are in your coven?"

"We are five witches and two warlocks. Of the seven of us, only four are natural witches and the rest have been taught because they had latent abilities. We need a powerful natural witch to lock in the final step of the spell."

It's a lot of information to take in at once but I am equal part scared and excited.

"Teach me. I am yours to mold."

"Have you ever used your firepower?"

"Not that I am aware of, but some things are starting to make sense now that I have more information."

She chuckles. "Okay. I want you to focus on the candle in front of you. Repeat these words until you can light the wick. *Illuminare noctem.*"

I stare at the pure white tapered candle, making sure to focus only on what I am doing.

"*Illuminare noctem.*"

The flame erupts immediately, dancing in the slight breeze coming through an open window.

"This is going to be easier than I thought," she says, impressed.

Chapter Sixteen

Korvin Slater

The Forest

Akasha and Krishka train together every day for two weeks. From what I understand, which isn't much, she is growing in strength by leaps and bounds. Krishka and I have called a truce and are even being civil to one another as we prepare for the storm that is coming.

Akasha is the lynchpin in their plan. Without her, the protection spell that will keep Aldron's brother out of Brooklyn cannot be cast. And today that spell will be cast.

I'm on edge about her doing this, knowing that anything could go wrong. My heat is thumping in my chest as I watch her sleep knowing that if anything happens to her, I wouldn't survive. My bear would go rogue, decimating anyone and everyone in its path until someone finally put me down.

"I can feel you staring," she mumbles, throwing her arm over her face.

"I'm not staring."

"It's creepy," she says looking at me with a frown. "If you wanted to wake me up you could always fuck me."

"I could fuck you either way."

I know she is using sex as a distraction, but I will allow it. It's not like being inside my mate is a chore by any stretch of the imagination.

Slowly, I pull the sheet down her delectable, curvy body, exposing her smooth caramel skin to my view. Her full breasts rise and fall with each breath, her nipples hardening beneath my gaze. I lick the tips, teasing them with my tongue until she is squirming beneath me.

"Korvin…"

"Shhh, Little Mate. You'll get what you want, you just need to be patient."

I run my fingers up the inside of her thigh until I find her entrance, gently pushing a single finger through her folds. I shallowly pump in and out of her pussy before withdrawing and rubbing circles on her already hardening clit.

"Harder," she demands, and I lighten my touch. She growls lowly and I chuckle at the sound.

"I want you to ride me," I whisper into her ear before sucking harshly on the lobe. "I want to watch your tits bounce as you take your pleasure."

"Yes," she hisses pushing me onto my back.

I grab her hips and pull her up my chest. "But first, I think you should ride my beard. I'll walk around all day with the smell of your pussy against my nose."

She stares down at me. We haven't done this before.

"I can't," she stammers. "My thighs are too big. What if I smother you?"

"Baby, you couldn't smother me if you tried, and I love these juicy thighs." I bite lightly at her left inner thigh. "But it would be a helluva way to die."

She shakes her head but allows me to position her where I want her. The moment my tongue touches her little clit, her insecurities are forgotten. I lick, suck, and nibble at her most intimate flesh while she fucks my face. Her hips move in tight little circles, chasing her pleasure, and all too soon her cream is coating my tongue as she moans her way through the first orgasm of the day.

Grabbing her hips, I lift her off my face mid-orgasm and lower her onto my erect cock. Her pussy spasms, gripping me as she throws her head back with a howl. Her nails puncture the skin on my pectorals as she holds on for dear life. Her hips shoot forward, fucking me in short thrusts as her orgasm peters out. I only allow her a moment of reprieve before I thrust into her from below.

"Fuck, that's pretty," I mumble staring at her bouncing breasts, entranced.

"How do you feel deeper like this?" she asks softly, lifting off my dick before impaling herself over and over.

Already I can feel my balls tingling with my impending orgasm, but I don't want this to end. My hand goes to the juncture where we are connected, and I rub harshly at her clit. Three more harsh thrusts and we both crash over the precipice into ecstasy.

****

It's fifteen minutes to midnight when we meet the Obsidian Coven in the woods, along with Aldron. I can feel the nerves of every person here as they prepare to do something monumental. Never in the history of New York has a coven taken on something as big as this protection spell.

Krishka has assured us that Akasha can handle this and even though I never liked her, I believe her. She has a fondness for my little mate and would never allow harm to come to her.

"Everything is set," one of the males in the coven says. All the witches enter the circle that has been carved into the earth.

I watch Akasha closely, so closely that I miss the threat, and by the time I realize what is happening it is too late. A sharp piercing pain shoots up through my back and my legs collapse. Around me, strange people that smell of death. Aldron is fighting three men but clearly losing.

My mate stares at me with tears streaming down her cheeks as she screams words I cannot hear. My eyes grow heavy, and I struggle to keep them open. The last thing I see is a vibrant burst of purple before the world around me goes dark.

Chapter Seventeen

Akasha LaVey

The Betrayal

Nervous energy thrums through my veins as I join Krishka and her coven inside the sacred casting circle. Excitement shines in her eyes as she grins at me widely. I have been introduced to her coven before but none of us have bonded the way Krishka and I have.

Something in the air shifts and I look around to see what the hell is going on.

It takes me a moment to understand what I am seeing as Korvin goes down to his knees before falling onto his side. I never knew pain like this was possible, but I swear to everything that is holy, my soul feels like it is being ripped to shreds. I scream into the heavens, calling his name over and over as I try to run to him.

A man wraps his arm around my neck from behind, covering my mouth with his other hand.

"Don't say a fucking word, Witch."

Tears stream down my face. Korvin stares at me with regret in his eyes and I want to tell him everything will be all right. But I can't. His eyes fall closed and I know my life will never be the same again.

I feel my magic surge up inside me and I want to decimate anyone and everyone around me that brought this tragedy to my door.

"I'm sorry, Krishka," a man named James says to her, catching my attention.

"You're sorry? You're fucking insane!" she yells being held back by a strange man of her own. "Look at her!" She points at me. "If any of us make it out of here alive, we'll be fucking lucky."

The man takes me in, and I see the fear in his gaze.

"At least have enough balls to tell me why you did it. What did Lucius offer you that made you think it was a good idea to murder the fucking mate of the most powerful natural witches on the fucking continent?"

"Um…"

"You complete waste of space!" she yells glaring at him as she fights the man that holds her. "You did it for money, didn't you."

I don't wait for his answer, the look on his face is all the confirmation I need. My anger and my magic surge and swell in unison. I feel full to the point where it explodes out of me. Howls of pain and terror ring out through the forest and the scent of burning flesh permeates the air.

One minute, a man is holding me captive and the next I am free. Krishka stares at me in wonder and fear as I glare at anyone left standing. My gaze travels back to my mate and his ashen form and I run to his side.

"Help me!"

Krishka and three of her coven mates are beside me in a heartbeat. Each of us have our hands buried in the dark soil of the earth and placed on his body as we push our magic into him, taking from Gaia herself to replenish what we lose so we have more and more to give.

It feels like an eternity before he moves, opens his eyes, and looks around. Aldron moves in behind him to remove the blade from his back as we continue to heal as fast as we can.

"He's alive," Krisha says. "But if you don't stop now, you won't be."

I stare at her wanting to deny her words but already I can feel myself waning. She takes my hands in hers and helps me up from the ground.

"Breathe. Watch your mate."

Turning to him, I see his prone form shift from man to bear. His animal seems disorientated and shakes his head as he stumbles to his feet, almost falling but regaining his balance in an instant.

The big black bear growls lowly, taking in everyone around us before walking toward me. He shoves Krishka out of the way and nuzzles into my side, scenting me and rubbing his smell all over my body. Through the tears that are streaming down my face, I can't help but laugh at his pure alpha bullshit.

****

It takes three hours for Korvin to shift back but when he does, weakness overwhelms him once more. Aldron helps me get him back to the truck while the coven clears the forest of all evidence that anything happened here tonight.

I drive us through Brooklyn and once we arrive back at the building that houses The Gin Room, the twin Minotaurs are there to help me get my mate back to our apartment. They lay him on the bed, and I thank them both for their help.

"Will he be okay?" Knox asks.

"He'll be out for a week or so, just like you were. But he'll be fine."

"I'm glad you were there. We like having his grumpy ass around," Cruz says with a grin.

Both of them hug me and tell me to call if I need anything before disappearing back into the elevator. I return to the bedroom where I use a damp cloth to clean the worst of the dirt and blood from my mate before I climb into bed beside him. Throughout the night, I pour little bits of love and magic into him, willing him to heal faster.

All I want is for him—and his bear—to be back to normal once more.

Chapter Eighteen

Korvin Slater

What Happened

I wake up ready to go to war. The only thing I remember is seeing my mate being held back as tears stream down her face. I can't get the image of her utter heartbreak out of my mind.

"You're awake."

I turn my head to see Krishka standing in the doorway. I frown at her, rubbing at the pain in my chest. If she is here, certainly something terrible has happened to my mate.

"Relax," she says with a smile. "Akasha will be back any minute. She's just strengthening her protection wards. It was my turn to watch you."

"How…" the words get lodged in my dry, scratchy throat.

She steps into the room and hands me a sealed bottle of water as I slowly push myself upright. Drinking the entire bottle, I take in the room around me. Gone is the white bedding and curtains, replaced with turquoise finishings. A selfie of Akasha and myself on our first day exploring the city has been blown up and framed to hang against the wall opposite the bed. I knew she would bring her personal touch to this apartment and make it our home.

"How long have I been out?" I ask returning my attention to the witch.

"Seven days. I wasn't sure you were ever going to wake up, but Akasha was adamant."

"Sounds like her."

I hear the front door open and moments later my beautiful mate is standing in the doorway, a brilliant smile spread across her face.

"Hey," her voice is soft as she stares at me.

"Come here," I command, opening my arms to her. She is in my arms in an instant.

I see Krishka leave and hear the door close behind her. My mate kisses my face all over before landing on my lips.

"I was so afraid."

It's only then that I realize she is crying. I hold her tightly and allow her to let out her emotions. I too have felt the fear of almost losing her and I would never diminish her feelings. I wish there was something I could do to make her feel better but all I have to offer is my love.

After long minutes of crying, she pulls back to look at me.

"How are you feeling?" she asks.

"Good. Not at all like I've been sleeping for seven damn days," I answer honestly.

"What happened?"

"We were betrayed." I can feel the anger roll off her in waves as her magic starts to gather. "One of the vampires who attacked us stabbed you in the back and severed your spinal cord."

"Fuck," I curse, thinking what kind of toll this must have taken on her. Knowing her, she could have died trying to heal me.

"I'm fine," she cuts in, like she can read my damn thoughts. "The coven helped me, and everyone has been taking turns healing you."

I nod. "What about the vampires?"

She blushes deeply. "I thought you were dead," she whispers. "It felt like my soul was being ripped to shreds and I just lost it. Krishka says the pain and anger unlocked the last of my hidden power. Basically, I turned everyone that wasn't on our side to ash."

"Damn, Little Mate," I say with a whistle. "Seems you're dangerous."

She laughs and I love the sound. It's so much better than her tears. "Only to anyone who wants to hurt the people I love."

"Then I'm glad to be on your good side."

I kiss her deeply. My bear is stomping around in my mind demanding we solidify the bond with our mate.

"You're still healing," she says when I palm her breast.

"I'm fine," I mumble between placing kisses on her neck. "I need to feel close to you, to know we are both here and safe."

She cups my face in her hands, assessing me closely before she speaks. "Fine. But I don't want you overexerting yourself."

I grin. "I'll behave, promise."

I don't give her any more time to object. Sliding the thin straps of her pretty yellow sundress down her arms, I bare her naked breasts to my gaze. My lips lock around a nipple and already my mate's hips are pushing down on my growing erection.

I want to take my time and worship my woman but the need to feel her pussy around my cock is driving me crazy. Slipping my hand beneath her dress, I grab her panties and tear them from her body. A loud moan falls from her lips as I fight to get the covers out from between us before I pull her down on my erection harshly. I hold her still, enjoying the feel of her around me, our bodies entwined just like our souls.

"Fuck, this is the best feeling in the world," I mutter between kisses and nips to her exposed chest.

"Ride me, Little Mate."

She doesn't need to be told twice. My mate fucks me hard, lifting her entire weight off my cock before taking me inside her once more. Her breasts bounce freely as she moans and drives me to the edge.

It only takes mere moments for both of us to reach our peak, but it is perfect. Later, I'll make love to her slowly.

Epilogue

Akasha LaVey

One Year Later: A New Development

We are back in the forest, standing in the clearing where everything changed. Beside me, my mate, and Krishka my mentor. Every full moon we come back here to strengthen the protection wards I have placed over Brooklyn.

Aldron's brother is still trying to get in for no other reason than to destroy what his brother built. I've come to realize the siblings have no love lost between them.

"Are you ready?" I ask Krishka.

"Always," she replies with a brilliant smile.

I take her hands in mine while Korvin watches over us, drawing on the magic all around us. Gaia provides everything I need to keep the powerful spell working but Krishka is my anchor. From the first time I cast the spell, she has been by my side making sure I don't overexert or deplete myself.

I am the only person that can keep the protection ward charged and no one wants anything to happen to me. I appreciate everyone caring about me, but I know in my heart I will be fine, Krishka is just a backup. And something my mate demands.

The moment the magic swirls around us, Krishka's eyes shoot wide. I shake my head with a smile, hoping she understands. I knew the moment we did this she would be able to tell that I'm pregnant, but I wanted to do the wards before I told Korvin.

He is going to be even more overprotective, and I

know he wouldn't be happy with me using this much energy during the first month of my pregnancy. I'm not worried. I know our son will be born strong and healthy, my natural magic and his father's shifter magic keeping him safe.

"By moon's embrace and winds that guide, guard this town, with strength and pride. Ancient roots, in earth entwined, shield the souls, from harm confined. Bound by light, bound by stone, let no ill through this ward be known."

The incantation falls from my lips without effort.

My magic swells around us before spreading out and blanketing Brooklyn. I smile as I release Krishka's hands, and she hugs me tightly.

"I'll see you tomorrow," she whispers with a wink before disappearing between the trees.

"Where is she going?" Korvin asks.

"Just giving us some privacy."

"Sounds interesting," he jokes with a raised brow. "Is my mate in the mood for some outdoor fucking?"

"I could be convinced," I say with a chuckle. "But first, we need to talk."

"Is there something wrong?" he asks, stepping closer to me.

"Not at all," I say placing my hand over my abdomen.

He watches my movement, a look of shock crossing his features. "Really?"

"No, I'm making a joke," I say sarcastically, rolling my eyes.

In an instant I am locked in his embrace as he kisses me. "I love you," he says once he pulls away.

"And I love you too, Grumpa."

The End

EVERNIGHT PUBLISHING ®

www.evernightpublishing.com